Roxy Hunter

and the Mystery of the Moody Ghost

By Tracey West

Based on the television movie screenplay
by Robin Dunne and James Kee

A Price Stern Sloan Junior Novel

PSS!
PRICE STERN SLOAN

PRICE STERN SLOAN
Published by the Penguin Group
Penguin Group (USA) Inc., 375 Hudson Street, New York, New York 10014, USA
Penguin Group (Canada), 90 Eglinton Avenue East, Suite 700, Toronto, Ontario
M4P 2Y3, Canada (a division of Pearson Penguin Canada Inc.)
Penguin Books Ltd., 80 Strand, London WC2R 0RL, England
Penguin Group Ireland, 25 St. Stephen's Green, Dublin 2, Ireland
(a division of Penguin Books Ltd.)
Penguin Group (Australia), 250 Camberwell Road, Camberwell, Victoria 3124, Australia
(a division of Pearson Australia Group Pty. Ltd.)
Penguin Books India Pvt. Ltd., 11 Community Centre, Panchsheel Park,
New Delhi—110 017, India
Penguin Group (NZ), 67 Apollo Drive, Rosedale, North Shore 0745, Auckland,
New Zealand (a division of Pearson New Zealand Ltd.)
Penguin Books (South Africa) (Pty.) Ltd., 24 Sturdee Avenue, Rosebank,
Johannesburg 2196, South Africa

Penguin Books Ltd., Registered Offices: 80 Strand, London WC2R 0RL, England

Library of Congress Cataloging-in-Publication Data

West, Tracey, 1965-
Roxy Hunter and the mystery of the moody ghost / by Tracey West.
p. cm.
"A Price Stern Sloan junior novel."
"Based on the television movie screenplay by Robin Dunne and James Kee."
ISBN 978-0-8431-2663-1 (pbk.)
I. Roxy Hunter and the mystery of the moody ghost (Motion picture) II. Title.
PZ7.W51937Rox 2007

2007001037

10 9 8 7 6 5 4 3 2 1

Every haunted house has a story. If you look far enough into the past, you will find its beginning—a moment in time that changes the lives of everyone in the house. That moment is so powerful that it lives on over the years. It just won't go away.

That's what happened at the Moody Mansion on a dark night years ago. If you had been standing outside, this is what you would have seen . . .

The dappled light of the full moon shines on the old stone house. Inside the house, a pretty young woman listens to a song on the record player. Outside, a young man in an army uniform walks up to the front door.

The girl looks out of her window on the second floor. She waves and smiles. The young man waves back, then quickly walks up to the front door. He knocks loudly.

A gray-haired man answers the door. He scowls at the sight of his visitor.

"Sir, I've come to ask for your daughter's hand in marriage," the young man says.

The older man is angry. "Get off my property!" he growls.

But the young man does not take no for an answer. He pushes past the girl's father into the house. The man follows, slamming the door behind him.

Then a loud shotgun blast explodes in the night.

The young girl screams.

And the music on the record player keeps playing . . .

Every haunted house has a history. But over the years, that history can get mixed up. It takes a real detective to find the truth. Someone curious. Someone brave. Someone who will not stop until the truth is found. Someone with an uncanny sense of fashion.

Someone like Roxy Hunter . . .

Chapter One:

• • • A New Start • • •

Roxy Hunter stared out the window of her mom's SUV. A song from the 1940s played on the radio. Roxy hummed along.

Then the music turned to static, and the static became a new song as Roxy's mom turned the dial on the radio. It brought Roxy out of her trance.

"Mother, I was listening to that!" Roxy protested. Her mom, Susan, a pretty brunette in her early thirties, was humming along to the new music.

"Come on, honey, that's a little dated, even for me," Susan Hunter replied.

Roxy frowned, wrinkling her nose. She adjusted the hat that covered her long, blond hair.

"Do you realize these are my last few moments to listen to NPR before I'm culturally ostrichized?" Roxy asked.

"Ostra-*cized*, dear," Susan corrected her. "Anyway, I promise you, you are going to love Serenity Falls. There's a lot to do there. It's a beautiful little town."

"And how am I going to live without the opera, museums, Broadway, long walks in Central Park?" Roxy asked. She sighed dramatically. "You can take me anywhere, but my heart will always belong to the Big Apple."

Roxy gave her head a little shake. Her red apple earrings dangled from her ears. She had worn them as a tribute to her favorite city. Who knew when she would ever see it again? Especially now that she was being forced to move to the middle of nowhere.

"Roxy, we lived in New Jersey," her mother pointed out. "You've been to Manhattan twice."

Roxy turned to face the backseat. Her friend Max, as usual, had his nose in a book. Max was a certified genius and was always studying.

"Can't your parents do anything about this, Max?" Roxy asked. "Save us from being moved to Siberia?"

Max just shrugged and kept reading. He was used to Roxy asking him countless questions daily.

Roxy turned back to her mom. "I'm going to

be a teenager soon, you know. Don't blame me if I end up a reclusive misfit."

"You're not going to be a teenager for three and a half years," Susan reminded her.

Roxy looked at Max again. "It looks like we have no choice but to get married now, Max. All we have is each other."

Max blushed. He was three years older than Roxy. A few years ago, she had decided they were destined to get married one day. That was something he was definitely *not* used to.

Max covered up his embarrassment the way he knew best—with information. "According to the last census, the population of Serenity Falls and its surrounding area is 8,519," he said, pushing his glasses up on the bridge of his nose. "Statistically speaking, that means there are quite a number of people in our age group."

At that very moment, the car turned off of the highway. A sign on the road in front of them read WELCOME TO SERENITY FALLS. POPULATION, 8,784.

"I stand corrected," Max said. "The odds just improved."

"That makes me feel *so* much better," Roxy said. But her voice showed she didn't mean it.

Soon they were driving through the center

of the town. Roxy looked out the window, curious. She could see that her mom's dark eyes flashed with excitement. Susan's brown hair bobbed on her shoulders as she craned her head to get a better look.

"Look at this place! Oh my gosh! It's adorable!" Susan said, grinning enthusiastically.

Old-fashioned lampposts lined the town's main street. Small shops sold everything from antiques to candles.

"Look at that!" Susan cried. "A wool shop! When was the last time you saw a wool shop?"

"About the same time I saw some really cold, naked sheep," Roxy mumbled, grumpy. She didn't see what was so exciting about this place. There was no way it could be better than their home in New Jersey.

Susan's excited smile faded. "I'm officially requesting an attitude change."

"Noted," Roxy said. "But only on the condition that I don't have to share your excitement for tourist traps."

Susan sighed. "You're far too young to be this cynical."

They drove through town. Soon the buildings and houses became fewer and farther between. They stayed on a tree-lined road for a while until they came to the entrance of a driveway.

They turned into the drive and passed more trees. Then the trees thinned to reveal a huge stone mansion, with towers jutting out of the red-tiled roof.

Roxy, Susan, and Max stared silently at the house in disbelief as Susan parked the car.

"Are you sure this is it?" Roxy asked finally.

Susan glanced at a piece of paper in her hand. "Thirty-two Greenwood Lane. The estate agent said it was nice, but this is . . ."

"Awesome!" Roxy cheered. A smile lit up her face as she forgot all about how much she had planned to hate her new home. She quickly took off her seat belt and ran toward the house.

Susan and Max followed right behind her. They walked up to the front door together. The heavy wooden door creaked as Susan pushed it open. The place was dusty, and sheets covered all the furniture. But it still looked really cool. The rooms were huge with vaulted ceilings, and large gothic windows let the afternoon sunlight spill across the shiny hardwood floors. There was even a balcony with a curling wrought-iron railing on the second floor, overlooking the grand living room.

"I can't believe we get to live here," Roxy said in awe.

"Me neither," Susan added.

Max shook his head. "It certainly is impressive."

Roxy's mind raced as she looked around the house. There were so many new things to see, so many rooms to explore. She couldn't wait to get started.

"Thank you for bringing us here, Mom," she said, hugging Susan.

"You won't mind living here, then?" Susan asked.

Roxy smiled. Her bad mood had melted right away.

"I'll manage!" she said, laughing.

Chapter Two:
· · · Bullies and Bumps in the Night · · ·

Susan, Max, and Roxy spent the afternoon unloading boxes from the trailer attached to the SUV. Max was carrying the last few boxes into the house as the sun began to set.

Roxy's head was filled with thoughts about the old mansion. Who had lived here before them? She imagined ladies in beautiful ball gowns and men in tuxedos. Maybe a quartet of musicians, playing a lively waltz. She danced around the front yard with an invisible partner.

"Oh, Max, what times we shall have here," she said, in her best snooty voice. "Can't you just see it? Tea in the garden, lawn bowling, croquet. And the dances . . . hey! Why don't we have an eggnoggural ball?"

"*Inaug*-ural ball," Max corrected her, but

before he could say more a soccer ball came flying through the air. It hit Max right in the head.

Max stumbled, but he didn't fall. Roxy ran to his side.

"Are you okay?" Roxy asked.

"Fantastic," Max said flatly, as a boy on a bike rode toward them. He was flanked by twin boys with twin smirks on their twin faces. The twins both had bright red hair and wore jeans, white T-shirts, and matching denim jackets. All the boys were laughing.

Roxy turned to the boys. "Hey, what's your problem?" she asked.

"Oh, I'm sorry," the first boy said sarcastically. "The ball slipped. Is your boyfriend going to cry?"

"He's not my boyfriend," Roxy said, her fists clenched in anger. "He's my *fiancé*, and you better be sorry, 'cause he's a Duck Chin Chu Ninja!"

"What?" The boy laughed. He didn't know what to make of Roxy.

"He was raised by the Wutan masters of Indonesia who taught him the secret art of Oriental brain kicking," Roxy answered matter-of-factly. She picked up the soccer ball. "He could snap your brain in two with our secret kick. Like this . . ."

Roxy gave the ball a mighty kick. The boy barely managed to catch it. The red-haired twins looked at each other and frowned.

"That's baloney," they said at once.

Roxy stared them down. "Okay. Find out the hard way. I dare you."

The boy almost looked like he believed Roxy. Then he turned to Max. "Is she making that up?"

"Yes," Max answered honestly. He wasn't afraid of bullies, but he didn't have much time for them, either. "What do you want?"

"You moving in?" the boy asked.

Max turned to look at the trailer and the boxes. "Whatever gave you that idea?"

The boy's eyes narrowed. "How old are you?"

"Twelve," Max answered.

The bully looked triumphant. "Well, I'm thirteen. Remember that."

"Traditionally, it follows," Max agreed.

The boy thought for a minute. He had expected the new kids to cry, or fight, or run away like new kids usually did. But these two were different.

"I'm Seth," he said finally. "This is my 'hood. That's Timmy and Tommy. They're twins."

"Twins? I never would have guessed," Roxy chimed in. "Does your mother dress you alike on purpose, or did you choose that look yourselves?"

Seth snorted, wanting to laugh in spite of himself. Roxy was pretty funny. But he couldn't just let her talk to his friends that way. "You know, the Moody Mansion is haunted," Seth said, trying to scare Roxy. "That's why nobody has lived there for years—until you dweebs moved in."

"The Moody Mansion?" Roxy had no idea the house had such a romantic name.

"Yeah, they say you can hear a ghost moving around in there," Seth replied.

With that, he nodded to Timmy and Tommy and rode down the road. The twins scowled at Roxy and Max before they turned their bikes and quickly followed.

"Good luck sleeping tonight, losers!" Seth called behind him.

If Seth had been trying to scare them, he had failed miserably.

"Haunted! Perfect!" Roxy said, looking at the house with anticipation. Ghosts were even more exciting than fancy dress balls and croquet!

So the ghosts took up residence in Roxy's busy mind for the next few hours. She and Max began unpacking dishes in the kitchen, but soon Roxy was staring out the window, daydreaming. A large hawk sat on a tree branch outside the window. It looked at Roxy quizzically, then flew away. Roxy grinned. Her new house was so cool!

"Wow! Maybe a murder happened here," Roxy said, thinking out loud. "And now the ghost has returned from the grave to wreath its revenge."

A horrible thought came to her. "Max, what if the ghost mistakes us for the killer?" she wailed, clutching Max's arm dramatically.

"Roxy, first of all, it's *wreak*, not *wreath*. And secondly, there is no empirical evidence to support the belief in ghosts," Max replied.

Roxy wasn't sure what "empirical" meant. But she figured that Max definitely didn't believe in ghosts. That was exactly like Max, Roxy thought. His brain was all facts and no imagination. That's probably what happened when you were a genius, she reasoned.

Just then, the sound of footsteps filled the kitchen.

"Max, listen!" Roxy cried. "The footsteps of the damned!"

But it was just Roxy's mother coming up from the basement.

"Well, I've got some good news and some bad news," Susan said.

"The bad news is the furnace isn't working."

Roxy shivered. There was definitely a chill in the air.

"And the good news?" Roxy asked.

Susan smiled. "I have a fun solution."

· · · ♥ · · ·

Soon they were settled in front of the living room fireplace, where a toasty warm fire burned. Roxy and Max snuggled into their sleeping bags. Susan lay on the couch. She held up a flashlight so they could see one another. The three of them were playing a favorite guessing game.

"Wait, wait, don't help me," Roxy said. "Russia?"

"Russia's not a continent," Max replied.

Roxy gave up. "Okay, then what's the sixth continent?"

"Australia," Max said.

Roxy was puzzled. "Australia's an island! How could it possibly be a continent, too?"

"It just is," Max said.

"That's just plain selfish," Roxy said, frowning.

Susan smiled, stroking her daughter's long hair. "Should we revoke its status, honey?"

Roxy nodded. "I think it's only fair."

"I'll get right on that," Susan assured her. She turned to Max. "Speaking of distant locations, we'll call your mom and dad tomorrow, to let them know you're all right."

Max saddened slightly at the mention of his parents. Their job as archaeologists took them all over the world. Sometimes they were gone for months and months at a time, and he missed them terribly. If it weren't for the Internet, he'd never be able to keep track of them.

"They're not in Kazakhstan anymore," Max said.

"What?" Susan was surprised. "Where are they?"

"Turkmenistan, trying to ship the relics back to the university," Max explained. "It's okay. They trust you."

"That's not the point," Susan said. "I'm sure they'd love to hear from you."

Max turned to look at the fire. "I guess," he said quietly.

Roxy was still thinking about continents. "What's the seventh continent?" she asked.

Susan yawned. "You'll have to find out tomorrow, my dear."

"You can't possibly be serious!" Roxy protested. "You're not going to tell me? However shall I sleep?"

"I feel your pain, but you know the game," Susan told her. "Good night."

She turned off the flashlight and rolled over. Roxy looked at Max.

"Completely unfair," she whispered. "How about a clue?"

Max sighed as he slipped off his glasses and closed his eyes. "It's an island as well."

Roxy bit her lip as she thought. "Long Island? Rhode Island? Hawaii?"

"Good night, dear," Susan called from the couch.

"Ireland? Iceland? Iceland! No, Greenland!" Roxy was sure she had it.

"Good night, Roxanne," Susan said sternly.

Roxy plopped her head down on her pillow. "Absurdly unfair!"

She closed her eyes, but her brain kept thinking about islands as she drifted off to sleep. Islands that could be continents. Really big islands . . .

Roxy began snoring and rolled over. Everyone slept peacefully as the night wore on and the fire slowly died down to smoldering coals.

. . . ♥ . . .

Suddenly, Roxy awoke from a dream. "Antarctica. Is that an island?"

Max snored gently in reply. She had been asleep for some time.

"Max, is it Antarctica?"

THUNK!

The loud sound startled Roxy. She froze, her heart pounding in terror. The sound had come from upstairs somewhere.

"Mom? Max? Mom? You awake?" Roxy hissed.

Then there was another sound—the sound of heavy footsteps. They were definitely coming from upstairs.

Roxy pulled the sleeping bag over her head. She closed her eyes tightly.

She wasn't thinking about continents anymore.

She was thinking about ghosts . . .

Chapter Three:
· · · Rebecca to the Rescue · · ·

"I'm telling you, it was a ghost!" Roxy said emphatically.

Roxy had spent a restless night in her sleeping bag. Now everyone was awake and gathered in the kitchen. Max flipped pancakes on the stove, Roxy was putting some sliced bananas in the blender to make a smoothie, and Susan was frantically searching the phone book for a babysitter. She was getting ready to start her brand-new job at Middleton Trust—Serenity Falls's one and only bank.

"Honey, there are no ghosts in this house, okay?" Susan said. She held the telephone in one hand, and she sounded flustered.

"Oh, really? Were you the one who was too terrified to sleep all night?" Roxy asked dramatically. "Have you any idea what sleep deprimation does to a child my age?"

"It's sleep *deprivation*, Roxy," Max whispered.

"Roxy, please!" Susan pleaded. "This is the last babysitter in the book."

"I don't need a babysitter!" Roxy protested. "Max and I will be fine by ourselves, thank you."

"Max has to study and you're too young to be left alone," Susan said.

Deep down, Roxy knew her mom was right. Even though Max was a genius, he studied at home through a school on the Internet. That kept him busy most of the time. And Roxy couldn't start at her new school until the next term. Still, she was certainly mature enough to look after herself, wasn't she?

"So you're going to leave me with some country pumpkin?" she asked her mother, trying to sound adult.

"Country *bumpkin*," Max corrected her.

"Whatever. I am perfectly capable of handling any situation!" Roxy said smartly. She pressed the button on the blender for emphasis.

But she had forgotten to put on the lid! Juice and banana bits splashed out of the blender, spraying all over the kitchen.

"Oops," Roxy whispered.

Max left his pancakes on the stove and grabbed a towel to help Roxy clean up. Susan just shook her head in frustration and sighed.

"Honey, you're driving me nutty," she said, forgetting that she was on the phone. "Oh, no, not you, Mrs. Slausen. What's that? You're available?" A smile of relief spread across Susan's face. Then she frowned. "Oh, not for a month? Well, I'll definitely call you then. Thanks, and bye." She hung up the phone and leaned against the wall, defeated, just as smoke began to pour from the pan on the stove. Max's pancakes were burning!

Max rushed to turn off the flame. "Sorry. Miscalculation."

Susan ran to the window and opened it, waving the smoke out into the crisp morning air. Then the front doorbell rang.

"Oh, great," Susan moaned. She hurried to the front door.

She opened it to find a cheerful-looking young woman with short blond hair standing there. She carried two cups of coffee and a paper sack in one hand.

"Welcome to Serenity Falls, Susan!" the woman said. She held out the coffee and the bag, which appeared to contain muffins. "We don't have a Starbucks, but I think you'll find Lenny's Coffee Shop does a much better job."

"Oh! Thanks." Susan politely took the breakfast. "But, um, who are you?"

"Rebecca," the woman smiled brightly. "Rebecca Robson."

Then it dawned on Susan. "Of course! The estate lawyer. It's nice to finally meet you. Listen, we can't believe this place. It's just so . . ." Susan trailed off, at a loss to describe the grandeur of their new home.

Rebecca nodded, smiling. "I know. You get a lot more bang for your buck out here in the country."

"Are you sure there hasn't been a mistake?" Susan asked nervously, knowing that, under normal circumstances, she's couldn't possibly afford such an elegant house.

"No, we're just renting it out to offset some of the legal fees from the Moody estate," Rebecca explained.

Rebecca followed Susan into the house. She glanced into the kitchen. Smoke still poured from the stove.

"One of those mornings?" she asked.

Susan nodded. "Oh, yeah. Roxy's not starting

school yet, I can't find a sitter, the pancakes are spilled, and the smoothie is burnt . . ." She shook her head. "I'm making no sense."

Rebecca smiled. "The house okay?"

"Yes . . . no . . . sort of," Susan replied. "The furnace isn't working."

"No problem," Rebecca said, "I'll get right on it!" She took off her jacket. Underneath she wore a paint-splattered pair of overalls and a tool belt.

Susan was impressed. "Wow. When you said on the phone you were getting the repairs done, I didn't think you were actually going to do them yourself."

Rebecca shrugged. "It's the kind of stuff you have to do until you make partner around here. But between you and me, I love it," she said. Then her brown eyes widened. "Hey! Why don't I watch the kids?"

Before Susan could answer her, a loud *thunk* came from the dining room, right next to the kitchen. The two women ran inside. A huge chunk of plaster was on the floor. Susan looked up to see a hole in the ceiling where the plaster had once been. Roxy ran in from the kitchen and stared, mouth agape, at the dust and debris covering the floor.

22

"Aha!" Roxy cried. "What more proof do you need? I declare this house officially haunted!"

"That's Roxy, my daughter," Susan told Rebecca. "Are you sure you don't mind babysitting?"

Rebecca laughed. "Not at all," she said. She nodded toward the mess on the floor. "Looks like I'm going to be here for a few days, anyway."

"You're a lifesaver!" Susan said gratefully. She turned to Roxy. "Honey, this is Rebecca from the law firm. She very kindly offered to babysit for you. Okay?"

"That depends," Roxy replied. She turned to Rebecca. "You believe in ghosts?"

"Absolutely," Rebecca said.

Roxy grinned. "Then welcome aboard!"

Susan looked at her watch. "Yikes! I'm late!" She grabbed her purse and headed for the front door. "Any troubles, call me at the bank. And thanks again, Rebecca."

She called out to Roxy as she hurried outside. "Be good, honey!"

"But of course," Roxy replied, waving from the doorway.

· · · ♥ · · ·

Susan drove to the bank as fast as she could—she didn't want to be late for her first day. Middleton Trust was a stately brick building in the center of town. She parked her car and ran toward the bank. A good-looking man with brown hair was sweeping the steps. He held the broom like a hockey stick, oblivious to Susan standing behind him.

"And Gretzky winds up! He shoots! He scores!"

Then he turned and saw Susan. Blushing, he opened the door for her. Susan smiled.

"Nice goal," she said. Then she stepped inside.

An older woman with a sour expression on her face greeted her in the doorway.

"May I help you?" she asked.

"Yes, I'm Susan Hunter," Susan replied.

"Oh, the new girl. I'm Mabel Crabtree," the woman said, without a hint of emotion in her voice. "You moved into the Moody Mansion. How nice for you."

Susan smiled. "Yes, it's really amazing!"

But the woman wasn't in the mood for conversation. "You're four minutes late," she snapped. "But I guess we can let it go as it's your first day."

Susan was taken aback. Obviously this woman

wasn't trying to make new friends. "Well, I'm really sorry . . ." she began.

The woman interrupted her again. "I'll get the assistant manager."

Susan looked around the bank. A few customers waited in line at the teller booths. It wasn't nearly as fast-paced or crowded as the bank where she had worked in New Jersey.

Then the hockey-playing sweeper walked up to her.

"Hello again," he said. "I'm Jon Steadman."

Susan laughed. "You're the assistant manager?"

Jon held up the broom. "Around here, 'assistant manager' means you get to do all the crummy jobs," he said. Then he caught himself, laughing nervously. "Not that *this* is crummy. Just . . . sweeping." He certainly hadn't meant to imply that talking to Susan was crummy.

As they talked, another man walked up. He looked like he was in his late fifties, and he had an outgoing smile on his face.

"Ah, Sandra Hunter," he said, extending his hand. "Our newest employee. Welcome to Middleton Trust. I'm Peter Middleton, but you can call me boss. Are you settling in all right?"

Susan shook his hand. "It's a little hectic, but we're managing. Thanks for putting us in touch with the estate lawyers. The place is incredible."

"Well, it's just been collecting dust since dear old Estelle passed away," Middleton said absently. "Glad we could find a use for it. Welcome aboard, Sandra."

He hurried off.

"It's *Susan*," Jon said, but not loud enough that Middleton could hear him. Susan and Jon laughed.

"Don't be too hard on him," Jon continued. "He's the head of the bank, mayor of the town, and justice of the peace. Our residential municipal multitasker."

"Wow," Susan said.

Jon grinned. "Now, let me show you around."

Chapter Four:

• • • The Secret Door • • •

While her mother explored the bank, Roxy and Max explored the yard around the Moody Mansion. Roxy did most of the exploring.

Max cast a worried look back at the house. "Roxy, I really have to be studying. My trig exam is tomorrow."

"Clues, Max, clues," Roxy said. "Do you think clues ever give a fig about trig—whatever that is? Now, Rebecca says that the lawyers look after this house because the owner, Estelle Moody, died years ago. Maybe she's the ghost."

"Why would she haunt the house?" Max wondered.

Roxy thought for a moment.

"Not even the dead like lawyers, Max," Roxy said solemnly.

27

She picked up a rusted piece of metal from the ground. "What is this?"

"I don't know," Max said flatly.

"Come on, you're the archaeologist," Roxy said.

"My parents are the archaeologists. I'm the twelve-year-old who's trying to get through grade eleven, remember?" Max said.

Roxy frowned and shook her head. "Really. I'm very disappointed in your powers of reduction."

"De-duction," Max said.

Roxy gave the yard one last look. "We've drawn a blank. Come on, Watson. Mom will be home soon."

"I hope she's making something good for dinner," Max replied. "I'm hungry."

They walked through the grass back to the house.

"Do you miss *your* parents?" Roxy asked Max.

Max shrugged. "Yeah," he answered.

Roxy was thoughtful for a moment. Her own dad had died almost three years ago. She still missed him every day.

"If I was a parent, I'd never leave my child. Not for one second," she said. "'Cause you'd never know if that was the last second you'd ever see them."

Max knew how much Roxy missed her dad. He was about to reply when something caught his eye.

"That window, up there," he said, pointing. A curtain fluttered through an open window on the top floor of the house. "It's open!"

Roxy started to get excited. This could be a clue! "That must be where the ghosts are getting in," she reasoned.

"Or the raccoons," Max added.

Roxy raced toward the house, galloping on an imaginary horse. "On, Windrunner!" she cried.

Max followed her inside (without an imaginary horse) as Roxy ran upstairs to the second floor. From the outside, it looked like the window was jutting out of the roof. There must be an attic or something above them. They just had to find an entrance.

"It's got to be here somewhere," Roxy said. She and Max walked up and down the hallways, opening doors. They had to find a staircase leading to the attic.

Roxy opened another door, which revealed a dusty storage room. Straight ahead was a set of stairs leading up.

"This must be it!" Roxy cried.

She bounded up the stairs with Max right

29

behind her. The stairs opened up onto a landing crowded with old junk.

"There's no door," Roxy said. "How did they get to the attic? Helicopter?"

"They must have sealed it off," Max guessed.

"Absurdly unfair," Roxy remarked.

They stared at the walls of the landing. A stack of large old paintings and photographs leaned against the far wall. Boxes were stacked haphazardly around the little landing.

Roxy walked over and started to tug open one of the boxes, but the old tape wouldn't give. She took a deep breath and pulled with all of her might. Suddenly, mid-pull, the box lid came loose, sending Roxy backward into the stack of paintings. The entire stack came crashing down on top of her.

"Roxy! Are you all right?" Max asked as he rushed over to help her.

Roxy pushed aside a few paintings, coughing as the dust settled.

"I think so," she answered. Max helped her to her feet, and they moved the last of the paintings aside. Finally, Max picked up the last painting.

"Roxy, look!" he exclaimed.

Hidden behind the painting was a tiny door locked with a padlock.

30

"Wow!" Roxy cried. They had found a secret door!

"This must be the way to the attic," Max said.

"Who lived here, hobbits?" Roxy joked.

"No, it's probably a crawl space," Max reasoned.

Roxy brushed her long hair away from her face. "We've got to break that lock off," she said, her voice determined.

But they didn't get a chance.

"I'm home!" Susan called from downstairs.

Roxy frowned. "You must swear to secrecy, Max. I invote the law of absolute, super silence."

Max sighed. "Roxy, it's *invoke*, not invote. And it's just a raccoon, not a ghost."

"Absolute super silence, Max!" Roxy insisted. "That's not me—that's the law."

• • • ♥ • • •

Downstairs, Susan looked around for the children.

"Hello? Anyone, hello?" she called out.

Then she noticed the basement door was open. She walked downstairs to see Rebecca prying at a vent on the ceiling with a wrench.

The bolt snapped with a loud crack. The vent opened up, and a bushel of black coal dust poured down on Rebecca, covering her head and shoulders.

"Oh! Are you all right?" Susan asked.

"I'm fine," Rebecca said, smiling to reveal a bright white smile against her black, dust-covered face. "Just over-torqued a nut. Did I get much on me?"

Susan laughed. "Yeah, a bit."

Susan helped Rebecca clean up the coal dust and then went upstairs to cook. After Rebecca left, Susan, Max, and Roxy had dinner. Max was as good as his word and kept the super silent secret of the attic to himself. He was used to Roxy's overactive imagination by now. And Roxy couldn't get into trouble just exploring the place, could she?

So Max fell asleep thinking about his trigonometry, not the ghost in the attic. He slept peacefully until . . .

Hoot! Hoot!

The sound of an owl woke Max. He looked at his clock and saw it was 1:15. He had to get some sleep for his test . . .

Klunk! A loud sound jolted him awake again.

It was definitely coming from the attic. Just like Roxy had said.

Thunk! There was another loud sound, and then the sound of footsteps. Footsteps coming right toward his room . . .

Creak! The doorknob began to turn. Max pulled the covers up to his eyes, terrified. The door opened slowly to reveal . . . Roxy, in her pajamas, clutching a teddy bear. Max relaxed.

"Did you hear that?" Roxy asked.

"Y-yes," Max said nervously.

"Operation Attic begins in the morning. We need to get the lock off of that door and search for the ghost," she said with fierce determination. "Try to get some rest." She left, closing the door dramatically behind her.

Max sighed, pulled the covers up over his head, and closed his eyes.

Chapter Five:

· · · Clues in the Attic · · ·

Roxy was ready to start investigating as soon as she woke up in the morning. But first she had to put on her magnifying-glass earrings. Roxy always felt that the first step to a successful investigation was the right accessories.

Then she picked up a toy walkie-talkie on her dresser. It wasn't exactly high-tech, but it would do the trick. She pressed a button on the walkie-talkie.

"Accessorization phase complete," she said. "Has Eagle One de-nested?"

She let go of the button and waited for a response. None came.

Roxy tried again. "This is Winnie the Pooh. Do you read, Piglet? Has Eagle One de-nested?"

She waited again, but got no answer.

Frustrated, she left the room.

She found Max in the study a few minutes later, sitting in front of his computer. He had his walkie-talkie next to him, but it was switched off.

"What are you doing? We have a mission to extracute!" she cried.

"It's *execute*, not extracute—and I have to be online in an hour to take my exam," Max said.

Then Susan walked into the room, putting in an earring. "Hey, honey. Max has a big test today."

Roxy faced her mother with her most innocent smile. "Yeah, Ma. I was just asking if he wanted anything."

"He probably wants to be left alone," Susan said as she walked away.

Roxy turned back to Max. "We all want to be left alone, but there's a certain ghost who won't let us. Isn't that right, Maxie?"

Max shivered at the mention of the ghost. He didn't believe in them, of course. There had to be some logical explanation for what was happening.

And the sooner they found that explanation, the better he would sleep . . .

• • • ♥ • • •

Back in the kitchen, Susan got ready to leave for work. Rebecca was already working on the house. She stood on a ladder, plastering the hole in the ceiling.

"Listen, Rebecca, I feel like I'm totally taking advantage of you here," Susan said. "Please let me pay you for babysitting."

"No, not at all. They're little angels," Rebecca said, flashing one of her sunny smiles.

"Well, thanks, but aren't we keeping you from all your lawyering?" Susan asked.

Rebecca stepped down from the ladder. "I don't mind. It's slow right now, and I'll be honest with you. I'm kind of depressed," she said. Her voice sounded sad. "It's my birthday on Saturday, and I don't really have anyone to celebrate it with, so keeping busy helps. You know?"

Susan nodded. "Depressing birthdays. I know that one." Then a thought came to her. "Listen, why don't you have dinner with us on Saturday?"

"Oh, I couldn't," Rebecca protested.

"We were going to have a big housewarming dinner, anyway," Susan insisted. "We'll make it a combo celebration. What do you say?"

Rebecca smiled. "That would be great. Thanks!"

Susan looked at her watch. "Gotta run! Don't want to be late again!"

. . . ♥ . . .

From the window in the study, Roxy watched her mother drive away. She turned to Max.

"Let's rumble," she said.

The two of them quietly headed to the secret door. Roxy held a crowbar she had swiped from Rebecca's toolbox earlier. She handed it to Max.

He used the crowbar to pry open the padlock. He slid it under the metal plate, pulling with all his might. He moved the crowbar around, slowly loosening the metal. Then, suddenly, the lock popped off and fell to the floor with a clunk.

Roxy pulled open the door. The old hinges creaked in protest. She shone her flashlight through the door. A crawl space filled with cobwebs and darkness lay ahead of them.

"A porthole into the unknown," Roxy said.

She crawled into the passageway. Max followed. They crawled a short distance until they came to another door. This one pushed open easily. Roxy climbed out of the crawl space and gasped.

The attic was a huge space crammed with old furniture, trunks, and boxes. It looked like some kind of museum—a museum filled with secrets. Roxy immediately headed for a pile of old boxes.

"What exactly are we looking for?" Max asked.

"Clues, silly," Roxy replied. She began to root through one of the boxes, which contained a pile of old clothes.

Max headed straight for the open window. He looked outside and saw a thick tree branch just a few feet away. Then he looked at the windowsill—and found the evidence he needed. He turned back to Roxy.

"It's raccoons," he said. "There's fresh mud on the windowsill. This is where they get in."

Roxy put her hands on her hips. "Then where, pray tell, are they now?"

"We probably scared them off," Max said.

"So this is how you close the case of the attic ghost?" Roxy asked.

"No, this is how," Max said. He shut the window with a slam. "I gotta go take an exam."

He walked back toward the crawl space.

"You do that!" Roxy called after him. "You do that, nonbeliever! The truth is in here, Max. We ghost hunters can feel it in our bones."

Max just ignored her. Roxy shook her head and looked around the attic.

"The truth is in here," she said quietly.

An old, dusty gramophone caught her attention. Roxy had seen one before. It was a record player, but you didn't need to plug it in.

This one had a record on it. She put the needle on the record and then turned a crank. The record began to spin, and an old tune filled the attic.

Satisfied, Roxy looked around some more. One of the boxes was a pretty shade of purple. She opened it up and saw it was crammed with old letters, papers, and photos. They covered some white fabric. Roxy picked it up and saw it was an old wedding dress. Moths had eaten through the fabric, but Roxy could see it had been beautiful once.

"Hmm. Interesting," she said. She put it aside and looked through the box some more. Something silver caught her eye. She reached in and picked up a fancy ring. She held it up to the flashlight.

There was some writing on the inside of the ring: E.M. FOREVER. T.C.

"Wow," Roxy said. This definitely felt like a clue. She looked in the box again. This time, she saw a black-and-white photograph. It showed a picture of a beautiful but sad-looking young woman. Roxy looked at the back of the photo.

In faded ink were the words: ESTELLE. CHRISTMAS 1944.

Estelle. E.M. forever. The clues began to click into place in Roxy's mind.

The lady who died in the house was named Estelle Moody. So the Estelle in the picture must be Estelle Moody—E.M. This was her box, her dress, her ring! Roxy ran out of the attic, through the house, and burst into the study.

"I know who the ghost is! I've got proof!" she shouted.

"Roxy, please! The exam's in fifteen minutes," Max said.

"It's Estelle Moody," Roxy rattled on. "I found her engagement ring. But she never married if her last name was still Moody! Don't you see? She's come back from the dead to find her true love. Now all we need to do is find out who T.C. is!"

Max rolled his eyes. "Roxy, please! My exam..."

"Exam, shmexam! This is important!" Roxy cried. "We need to reunificate this lost love from the grave!"

"*Reunite*, not *reunificate*, Roxy!" Max called after her as she hurried off down the hall.

Chapter Six:

· · · Madame Roxy's Séance · · ·

While Roxy was busy coming up with a plan
to help the ghost of Estelle Moody, Susan was
getting used to her new job.

"There you go, Mrs. Taylor," Susan said,
handing a receipt to a customer. "And be sure to
bring me that carrot cake recipe next week."

Mrs. Taylor smiled brightly and left the
bank. Jon walked up to Susan.

"I'm impressed," he said. "Just one day and
you've mastered the art of small-town small talk."

"It's kind of nice," Susan said. "People are
actually interested in one another's lives here."

Then Susan noticed Mrs. Crabtree—the
sour-faced woman she had met on her first day—
coming toward them.

"Jon, if I'm volunteering at the food drive this evening, I'd like a list of qualified recipients," Mrs. Crabtree said.

"Uh, I'm sorry, Mabel, but Susan agreed to help me out," he said. "Being new here and all, I thought it would be a great way for her to meet some neighbors."

Jon turned to Susan and gave her a look that said, "Please go along with this." She understood.

"Yes," Susan said. "I thought it would be a nice way to say hi."

"I see," Mrs. Crabtree said. She eyed Jon and Susan suspiciously as she walked away.

Susan had an idea what the woman might be suspicious about. Yesterday, Susan had learned all of the rules and regulations of Middleton Trust— including the rule against employee dating. But this was just some volunteer work, wasn't it?

"Thanks for covering," Jon said gratefully. "You don't have to come. I just had to avoid spending the evening with Crabby Crabtree."

"I think it's a really nice idea," Susan said. "I'd love to help out."

Jon looked surprised. "Really?"

Susan nodded. "It sounds like fun."

Later, Susan called Max at home.

"Would you mind watching Roxy for a couple of hours tonight?" she asked. "I'm helping at a bank function. I should be home around nine."

"No problem, Mrs. Hunter," Max replied.

"Susan," she corrected him.

"No problem, Susan," Max said.

"You're an angel. See you later!" Susan said.

· · · ♥ · · ·

As Max hung up the phone, he saw something outside the window. Roxy was outside, along with Seth, Timmy, and Tommy.

Roxy was arguing with Seth. "Are too!"

"Am not!" Seth shot back.

"Are too!"

"Am not!"

"Are too," Roxy replied. "Stamped it, infinity, no erasees. You're chicken."

Roxy began to flap her arms and cluck like a chicken.

"You better cut that out, dwarfus!" Seth said angrily.

Max stepped out the door.

"Hey, look, it's your four-eyed boyfriend," Seth taunted.

"Fiancé," Roxy corrected him. She turned to

Max. "Hello, dear. I was just informing dimwit and the pumpkin heads that they're far too chicken to attend this evening's séance."

"Séance?" Max was beginning to regret his offer to babysit.

"Of course," Roxy said, as though Max should know everything about it. "Madame Roxanne Dupuis d'Hunterre will be attempting to contact the spirits of the long departed this evening."

"I am so *not* frightened," Seth said. "We'll be there. Right, guys?"

The twins looked nervously at each other.

"No way," said Timmy.

"That place is totally haunted," Tommy said.

"Last week our brother said he saw a light moving in the attic," Timmy added. "No way."

Roxy was interested. "A light?"

That didn't worry Seth. "I'm not afraid of some dumb ghost. I'll even spend the night in the attic!"

Roxy shook her head. "Very, very foolish words."

She looked up at the attic window. A brown hawk was perched on the roof just above it. The hawk let out a piercing cry.

"The call of the dead," Roxy said cryptically.

A look of terror crossed the twins' faces. They got on their bikes and pedaled away. Seth looked after them, doubt on his face. But he turned back to Roxy and Max.

"I'll be here," Seth said firmly.

· · · 💜 · · ·

It was dark by the time Roxy was ready for the séance. First, she needed the proper outfit. A shiny green tablecloth she found in the attic made a good robe. She tied it around her waist with the pink sash from her mom's bathrobe. She wrapped a metallic orange scarf around her head for a turban and put in her turquoise mirrored earrings. Then she looked at herself in the mirror.

She had to admit it looked pretty good. Her striped tights didn't exactly match her robe, but they added a colorful and mysterious touch. Satisfied, she headed downstairs.

The dining room would be her séance room. She unpacked the candles her mom used for dinner parties and set them around the room. She placed the engagement ring and the photo of Estelle Moody on the table. Then she turned off the overhead light and lit the candles.

"Just one more thing," Roxy muttered. She

ran to the study and looked through the boxes of books waiting to be unpacked. She didn't know much about holding a séance. But some good, ghostly words ought to help set the mood.

"Perfect!" she said, picking up a copy of *Macbeth*. The Shakespeare play was famous for its witches. She knew just the spooky words to say.

Finally, she was ready. She had Max and Seth sit at the table. Then she walked into the room dramatically, reading from the book. "Bubble, bubble, toil and trouble; fire burn and cauldron bubble . . ." she began.

Seth snickered. "What are you supposed to be?"

"Silence!" Roxy commanded. "Madame Roxy Dupuis d'Hunterre needs silence to conjure the lost souls of Moody Mansion."

"You couldn't conjure a burp," Seth said. He belched loudly, then laughed.

Roxy grabbed his arm. "I will not be responsible if you make fun of the dead, and they wind up haunting you and your descendants for hundreds and thousands of years," she warned.

That seemed to scare Seth a little. He didn't have a comeback. Roxy sat at the head of the table.

"Let us begin," she said, in her most serious

voice. "Come to us, oh spirit of the house. I command you!"

"Maybe you should ask nicely," Seth suggested meekly.

"Silence!" Roxy boomed. Then she froze in place. "Yes, yes, I feel the presence. By the great Magoo. By the Haley of comets, I command you!"

Roxy put the engagement ring on her finger.

"Show yourself, now!" she commanded.

Roxy held her breath, waiting for a response. Surely the ghost couldn't ignore *that*!

But nothing happened.

Seth and Max looked relieved.

"Told ya," Seth said. "You can't conjure no ghosts."

THUNK! At that exact moment, a chunk of plaster fell from the ceiling and crashed on the floor. Seth jumped in his chair.

"Aaaaah!" he screamed.

"That's not a ghost," Max explained. "That happens all the time."

"It is too the ghost!" Roxy cried. "It is too!"

Max shook his head. "Roxy, there's no such thing as—"

KA-THUMP! Another loud crash echoed

47

through the house. But this time, the noise came from the attic.

"What was that?" Seth asked.

"Just the raccoons getting back in," Max said.

"But you closed the window," Roxy pointed out.

Max looked up. He knew Roxy was right.

Then came another *THUMP!* Then a *CRASH!* And finally, a piercing scream . . .

"Aaaaaaah!" Seth screamed again, and this time, he bolted out of his seat. He ran for the front door without looking back.

But Roxy was excited, not scared. "My ghost trap! It got her! Come on!"

Roxy grabbed the flashlight next to her and ran up the stairs as fast as she could.

"Ghost trap? Wait! Roxy! Be careful!" Max yelled. He followed right behind her.

Roxy hurried through the crawl space. Earlier that day she had set up a ghost trap using strings, cans, and an old bedsheet. Now something was moving under the trap, moaning under flowing white sheets. Max emerged from the crawl space and stared in awe at the trap.

"It's a ghost," Roxy said, her voice hushed. "A real live ghost."

Chapter Seven:
• • • A Secret in the Attic • • •

Roxy and Max slowly inched forward. Max reached for the sheet with a shaking hand and pulled it back.

"*Aaaaaaah!*" A young man with messy black hair screamed at the sight of Max and Roxy.

"*Aaaaaaah!*" Max and Roxy screamed at the sight of the young man.

The man grimaced and rubbed his head. "Oooh, I think I hurt my head," he said in an East Indian accent.

"You're not a ghost," Roxy said, disappointed.

Max ran toward the crawl space. "Roxy, it's a burglar! Call the police!"

"No, please! I am not a burglar!" the man cried. "My name is Ramma! Ramma Vingri! I live here!"

Roxy and Max looked at each other.

"You live here?" they asked at once.

"I can explain," he said. "But, oh, my head!"

Roxy ran downstairs and got a bag of ice from the freezer. Max insisted on guarding Ramma. When Roxy came back with the ice he gratefully placed it on his head. Then he began his story.

"You see, I am just a poor medical student trying to survive my horrendous examinations," he said.

"How long have you been living here?" Roxy asked.

"Three months," Ramma replied. "Last term I was asked to leave my dormitory due to lack of funds. But I promised my mother and father that I would return home as Ramma Vingri, M.D. I thought my prayers were answered when I found this abandoned house. And when people began to come around I moved up here to live until I finished the tests."

"How did you get in and out without us seeing you?" Max asked.

"I would leave very early in the morning, and come back late at night, utilizing the trellis to climb in the window," Ramma explained. He rubbed his eyes. They were bloodshot from lack of sleep. "Pardon me, but I'm tired. These exams are exhausting."

Max nodded. "I know how you feel."

"You wouldn't believe it," Ramma went on. "Why, just yesterday I confused the temporal lobe with the occipital. Pretty soon I won't be able to tell my right foot from my left foot. And now that you've found me, I guess I won't be able to tell a nice, warm attic from a cold, lonely bus shelter."

Ramma sighed and stood up. He picked up an overstuffed backpack and slung it over his shoulder. He looked very sad.

"How long do you have left?" Roxy asked.

"Only one more week, thank goodness," Ramma said. "I am very sorry to have scared you. You seem like such nice children."

Ramma slowly walked toward the window. Roxy ran after him.

"Ramma, wait! You don't have to leave," she said.

Ramma turned around. His dark eyes were wide with surprise.

"Really?" he asked.

"Of course not! Right, Max?" Roxy said.

Max frowned. He wasn't sure how Mrs. Hunter would feel about a stranger living in the attic.

"I don't think your mom will go for this," he said.

"We don't have to tell her," Roxy said. "It'll be our secret."

Max bit his lip. Mrs. Hunter *definitely* would not like that.

"Come on, Max!" Roxy pleaded. "It's just for another week. We can't put him out on the street! Look at him!"

Ramma looked like a sweet, lost puppy. Max sighed.

"Pleeeeeease?" Roxy pleaded.

Max thought about it. It did seem kind of cruel to throw Ramma out. He gave in. "I guess . . ."

"Oh, thank you, thank you!" Ramma cried. "You are the kindest children to ever grace the earth with your presence."

Then a familiar voice rang through the house. "I'm home!"

"It's Mom!" Roxy cried. She turned to Ramma. "Remember, no stomping around!"

"Oh, no, I promise," Ramma said. "I will be as quiet as an elephant."

Roxy and Max stared at Ramma, confused.

Ramma grinned sheepishly. "An elephant with very small feet!"

Then Roxy and Max ran downstairs and

greeted Susan. She told them all about the food drive at the bank.

They didn't say a word about Ramma in the attic.

Soon it was time for Roxy to go to bed. She put on her pajamas. Then she looked at Estelle Moody's ring, which still shone on her finger. The story of lost love had been so romantic. But it looked like it was just a story. There was no ghost in the attic at all. Just Ramma.

Roxy took off the ring and placed it on the table next to her bed. Then she crawled under the covers.

"Another case closed by Roxy Hunter, supersleuth," she said with slight disappointment. She had really hoped the Moody Mansion was haunted. That would have been so cool.

Roxy drifted off to sleep, and Ramma kept his word. No more thumps or bumps came from the attic.

But sometime in the middle of the night, Roxy awoke to a different sound entirely—and it was coming from her room! Roxy slowly opened her eyes, scared of what she might find.

The hawk that she had seen earlier was

sitting on her bedside table! Roxy held her breath, not daring to move. The bird seemed to stare right through her with its golden eyes. Then it bent down and grabbed the ring in its beak!

The bird cocked its head, as though it wanted Roxy to understand something. Then it quickly flew off the table, through the window, and out into the night.

Roxy jumped out of bed and hurried to the window. She watched the hawk vanish into the darkness.

"Whoa," Roxy said in a hushed whisper. "I love this place!"

Chapter Eight:

· · · The Mysterious T. C. · · ·

Roxy couldn't wait to tell Max about the hawk. She found him in the study the next morning, working on his computer.

"The ghost is real, Max!" Roxy cried as she burst through the door. "A hawk came and took the ring in the middle of the night! Don't you see? The ghost wants the ring back!"

Max stood up and walked to the open door. He checked to see if anyone else was nearby. Then he shut the door and turned to Roxy.

"Roxy, there is no ghost, okay? It's Ramma," he said.

Roxy shook her head. "No, no, no. That was the Case of the Noise in the Attic. This is the Case of the Ghost of the Ring. Totally different. We have to find that bird immediately!"

"No, I have another exam today," Max said firmly. "I have to study. And then we have to figure out a way to tell your mother that we let a stranger sleep in her house without her knowledge. So no, chasing an imaginary bird is not on the itinerary!"

"What? I'm shocked, Max," Roxy said. "Truly. You lack an appreciation for the mysterious. We'll have to work on that."

Max opened the door. "Out. I have to study." Roxy couldn't believe it.

"So. This is what it comes to," she said slowly. "My own fiancé. Very well. I will go on, Max. But let me just say . . ."

Max didn't give Roxy a chance to finish. He gently pushed her through the doorway. "Out." The door clicked shut behind her.

Grumpily, Roxy headed for the kitchen. If Max didn't want to help, that was his problem. She would solve the case by herself. But first, she needed nourishment.

She found her mom and Rebecca in the kitchen.

"Honestly, I don't think I'm ready for dating," Susan was saying.

Roxy froze in the doorway. "Not ready for dating who?" she asked.

"Roxy!" Susan cried. She obviously hadn't heard Roxy coming. "Uh, nothing, dear. Nothing at all. Do you want some breakfast?"

Roxy frowned. *Why* would her mom be talking about dating? *Who* could she be dating after just a few days in town? She was about to question her mom when something caught her eye.

"The hawk!" Roxy cried. It perched outside the kitchen window. Once again, it seemed to be staring right at her.

Roxy ran out of the kitchen. She grabbed her jacket from the foyer.

"What are you doing?" Susan asked.

"Uh, nothing, dear, nothing at all," Roxy replied, mimicking her mother.

Then she ran out the door. Susan ran after her.

"Stay close to the house!" she called out. "That's an order! I'm still your mother!"

Roxy ran around the house to where she had seen the hawk. Now the bird was flying circles overhead. Roxy ran through the field behind the house, following it.

She ran until she came to an old wood fence. The hawk flew over the fence and into the woods.

Roxy looked back at the Moody Mansion. Her mom had said not to go far. But she could still see the house, couldn't she? And if she didn't follow the hawk now, she would never solve the case.

She made up her mind. Then she took a deep breath and climbed through the fence.

The hawk had landed on a tree branch in the woods. Roxy approached, and it flew ahead to another tree. She followed the hawk like this until they soon came to a small clearing in the woods.

Roxy gasped. Crumbling stone tombstones stuck out of the patchy ground. She was in an old cemetery!

The hawk flew past her and landed on what looked like a small stone house at the end of the cemetery. Roxy knew that it was a kind of tomb with a special name. Usually a bunch of people from one family were buried inside.

Roxy slowly approached the tomb. There was a name engraved over the door.

"Middleton," Roxy read out loud. "No way I'm going in there."

But the hawk had something else to show her. It flapped its wings and flew off of the

Middleton tomb. Then it landed on a headstone not far away.

Roxy ran up to it. As soon as she got close, the hawk flew away. Roxy was about to cry out when she noticed something on top of the grave.

Estelle Moody's engagement ring!

Roxy reached out and picked up the ring. Then she read the words on the headstone. "Lieutenant Theodore Caruthers. November 12, 1920–December 21, 1944. *Corpus inrepertus.*"

Roxy let the words sink in. Then something clicked. She looked at the inscription inside the ring.

"Theodore Caruthers. He's T.C.!" she cried.

This was big. She had found Estelle Moody's fiancé! But she needed to know more about him. And when you needed to know more, there was only one place to go: the library. Roxy headed out of the woods. Rebecca was busy fixing the house. Max was chained to his computer. Nobody would notice she was gone.

She headed for the center of town.

· · · ♥ · · ·

By the time Roxy reached the main street, it was lunchtime.

Susan and Jon had decided to take their lunch break from work together at Lenny's Coffee Shop.

"So listen, I've got to ask you a huge favor," Jon said. "Have you ever seen the film *An Affair to Remember*?"

Susan nodded. "Sure. Cary Grant."

"That's the one," Jon said. "It's my favorite movie."

"I'm fond of it, too." Susan smiled at Jon across the table.

"Well, it's playing tomorrow night at the review, and I desperately want to see it," Jon continued.

Susan had a feeling she knew where this was leading. "But?"

"But I can't go alone because of my condition."

"Condition?" Susan asked, concerned.

"If I go alone, I will cry," Jon said dramatically. Susan giggled.

"We're not talking a little sniffle, we're talking waterworks. It's very embarrassing. But if you're there, I'll be forced to attempt to appear macho."

He reached across the table and took her

hands in his. "No one will ever take me seriously as a banker if they discover what a wuss I am. Please?"

Susan laughed, then nervously pulled her hands away. "Well, if it's a mission of mercy, how can I say no?" she said shyly.

Roxy watched the whole scene from the street corner.

"Not dating? Right," she said, frowning. But the Case of the Dating Mom would have to wait. She crossed the street and walked to the town library.

Roxy marched right up the stone steps and straight to the checkout counter. There was no one behind the desk.

"Hello? Hello?" Roxy banged her hand on top of the desk. "Could I get some service?"

To Roxy's surprise, a man popped up from behind the desk.

"Shhhhh!" he said, putting his finger to his lips. Roxy jumped back. The man was very thin and wore a dark suit. His pale skin made him look like a statue in a wax museum.

"Did I frighten you?" the man asked.

"Yes," Roxy replied honestly.

"Good. Because you gave me quite a start.

One doesn't shout for assistance in the library, my dear child," the man scolded gently. "It is 'a cathedral of learning,' to quote St. Thomas Aquinas."

"One shouts for assistance when one can't find anyone to assist them, especially when they're having a really bad day, to quote Roxy Hunter!" Roxy shot back.

The man smiled at her quip. "I am Mr. Tibers, librarian. How might I assist you, Ms. Hunter?"

Roxy took a piece of paper from her pocket. She had written down the words from the headstone. She slapped the paper on the desk.

"I want to know what this means," she said.

The librarian looked at it curiously. "*Corpus inrepertus*. It's Latin. Meaning something to the effect of 'body not recovered.'"

Roxy looked thoughtful. "Body not recovered?" Then where *was* the body of Lt. Theodore Caruthers?

"And where did you reach such a mordant phrase?" Mr. Tibers asked.

"It was on a grave," Roxy replied.

"A grave. Of course it was," Mr. Tibers said. "Signifying that the body of whomever died is not buried there. Where did you find this grave?"

"A hawk showed me," Roxy answered.

The response did not seem to surprise Mr. Tibers. "A hawk. Interesting," the librarian said thoughtfully. "Native American lore has it that the hawk's cry pierces our fog of unawareness and asks us to seek the truth. They are the messengers of the spirit world."

Suddenly, everything made sense to Roxy. The spirit of Estelle Moody must be inside the hawk! "Of course they are."

"Quite. Is there anything else I might be able to assist you with, my most estimable Roxy Hunter?" the librarian asked.

"I need all the books you've got on Ted Caruthers," Roxy said.

Mr. Tibers looked puzzled. "Is he an author?"

"No, he's dead," Roxy replied. "I think he used to live in this town."

The librarian thought for a moment. Then he began to nod his head. "Wait a minute, the Caruthers family. Of course. They moved away long ago. Don't seem to remember a Ted. But we've got the *Serenity Falls Herald* archived. There might be something about him there."

Mr. Tibers showed Roxy how to use the

microfilm machine. She looked on a screen to see images of old pages from the newspaper. She used a round knob on the side of the machine to scroll through the pages.

Finally, she saw the name she was looking for.

"Mr. Tibers! Mr. Tibers! I found it!" she cried out.

The librarian came to her side. "You know, you really must stop shouting in the library. You're disturbing the other patrons," he said, but his voice was friendly.

Roxy looked around the library. "There's nobody else here."

"A mere technicality," the librarian replied.

"I found Ted Caruthers," Roxy said anxiously.

"Excellent! You're quite the sleuth," said Mr. Tibers. He leaned over Roxy's shoulder and began to read.

"County track star dies tragically when troop ship goes down in the Atlantic." He looked at Roxy. "*Corpus inrepertus.*"

Roxy thought about this. "Troop ship." That meant Ted Caruthers was in the military. He died at war.

Was that why he and Estelle Moody never got married?

"This demands further investigation," Roxy

64

said. She turned back to the machine.

"I'm afraid it will have to wait," Mr. Tibers told her. "It's already past closing."

Roxy looked at the clock. It was already after six o'clock! Her mom would be home any minute.

"Oh no!" Roxy cried.

She thanked the librarian and hurried home as fast as she could. As she ran up the drive to Moody Mansion, she saw a strange car parked in front of the house. Roxy ran up to the door and took off her jacket and shoes, ready to sneak into the house. She pushed the heavy front door open slowly, cringing at the loud creak it made. Then she heard her mom call her from the dining room.

"Roxanne, could you come here, please?"

"Roxanne? Not good," Roxy muttered. Her mom only called her Roxanne when she was really mad! Roxy walked into the dining room. Her mom sat at the table, along with that guy she had lunch with, Max, and one more person . . . Ramma!

"Uh-oh," Roxy said.

Chapter Nine:

• • • Plans and Promises • • •

"I can't believe you would do this," Susan said. Her expression was a mix of anger and worry.

"Please, Mrs. Hunter, this is all my fault!" Ramma blurted out.

"No, Ramma, it is not," Susan said firmly. She turned to Roxy. "Why didn't you tell me there was a stranger living in the attic? Do you have any idea how dangerous that could have been?"

"He's just a poor soul trying to get through medical school," Roxy said sheepishly.

"I'm sorry, Mrs. Hunter," Max said. "It's my fault, too."

"I know, Max," Susan said. "I'm really very, very disappointed in you two."

Roxy stared at the floor. Her mom wasn't finished.

"And then you go and disappear all day. I cannot believe you would do such a thing. I told you not to leave the property," Susan fumed. "Jon was about to go and look for you. Who knows what could've happened? You are grounded, young lady."

Roxy's eyes filled with tears. She ran out of the dining room and up the stairs to her room. She slammed the door behind her.

Downstairs, Ramma stood up. He looked like a lost puppy again.

"I think I have caused this family much grief," he said. "Once again I am very sorry."

He started to walk out of the room.

"Wait, Ramma!" Susan said. "Where are you going to stay?"

"A cardboard box, I imagine," he answered gloomily.

"Listen, I've got a spare bedroom," Jon offered. "You can crash with me."

Ramma looked confused. "I'm sorry. 'Crash'? Will I need a helmet?"

Jon smiled. "No. You can stay at my place for a while."

Now Ramma smiled, too. "Bless you greatly for your kindness!" he said. He turned to Susan and gave a slight bow. "Again, I am truly sorry for the inconvenience I have visited upon your family."

Jon stood up and steered Ramma toward the door. Ramma bowed once more.

"Once again, very sorry," Ramma said.

"I think they get it," Jon interrupted.

Susan left the dining room without saying a word to Max. Dishes overflowed the kitchen sink. She rolled up her sleeves and began to wash them. Before she knew it, tears streamed down her face.

Max appeared in the doorway.

"You okay?" he asked.

"Yeah, yeah," she said. "Just got some soap in my eyes. That's all."

She tried to stop crying, but the tears kept coming. "It's just kind of hard doing this alone. Sometimes it gets a little overwhelming. And . . . I think a lot about Roxy's dad."

"I understand," Max said. "I miss my parents, but they're only in Turkmenistan. They're not . . ."

"You can say 'dead,' Max," Susan said softly. "David died. It happens. It's not fair. It's lousy. It's really, really lousy. But it happens."

"Anyway, I can only imagine what you must be feeling," Max said. "I'm sorry for that."

"Thank you, Max," Susan said. She wiped her tearstained face with her sleeve.

"Not a problem," Max said. He turned to leave.

"Do me a favor?" Susan asked. "Don't let any more strangers sleep in the house, okay?"

She smiled, and Max smiled back.

"Okay, Mrs. Hunter," he said. Susan raised an eyebrow.

"I mean, Susan," he corrected himself.

Max left, and Susan finished the dishes. Then she walked upstairs to Roxy's room. The lights were off, but Roxy was lying on top of the covers. Her eyes were wide open.

"Hello," Roxy said.

Susan noticed a suitcase at the end of the bed.

"You leaving, honey?" she asked.

"Yes," Roxy said. "I thought it would be best for all of us if I was to go. If you'd be so kind, I'd like to wait until morning."

Susan smiled. "But you're grounded, sweetie. Were you planning on living at the end of the yard?"

"If need be," Roxy said stubbornly.

Susan sat on the edge of the bed. "Roxy, the reason I got so upset was that you left without telling anyone where you were. And you're too young to be going off into a strange town by yourself," she said. She reached out and gently stroked Roxy's hair. "Maybe I shouldn't have raised my voice, but I love you, sweetpea. You're my whole world. Okay?"

Roxy looked at her mom. "Are you going to marry him?"

Susan was surprised. "Marry? Who?"

"You know, him. That guy who was downstairs," Roxy said.

"Jon?" Susan laughed. "No, honey. He's just a friend from work."

Roxy wasn't buying it. "Do you make a habit of holding hands with friends?"

"Holding hands?" Susan asked.

"I saw you two at the restaurant," Roxy informed her.

Caught off guard, Susan shook her head. "Roxy, we were just goofing around!"

Roxy still didn't believe it. "Goofing. I see," she said, her voice cold.

"Sweetheart, I like Jon," Susan said. "He's a very nice man. But no one is going to replace your father. I will always love him."

Roxy softened a little. "Is it a love from

beyond the grave, like Estelle Moody and Ted Caruthers?"

"Who?" Susan asked.

"It's very complicated," Roxy said. "I don't have all the details. Just tell me it is."

Susan kissed her on the forehead. "I'll tell you this. No one is going to replace you in my heart. Ever."

"Promise?" Roxy asked.

"I promise," Susan replied.

"Promise?" Roxy asked again.

"I promise."

"Promise?" Roxy wanted to hear it again.

Susan sighed. "Roxy . . ."

Roxy smiled. "Third time's the charm, Ma."

Susan smiled back. "I promise."

She kissed Roxy one more time. Then she walked to the door. Before she left, she looked down at the suitcase.

"Will you be staying with us, then?" she asked.

"Am I still grounded?" Roxy countered.

"Yep," Susan answered.

Roxy rolled over on the bed. "I'll take it under consideration."

Susan looked fondly at her daughter. Roxy

was stubborn and a little too smart for her own good. And Susan wouldn't change a single thing about her.

"Good night, Roxy," she said.

"Good night, Mom," Roxy replied.

Chapter Ten:
· · · The Plot Thickens · · ·

The next day, a sort of peace fell over the
Moody Mansion. Roxy promised not to leave the
grounds, and Susan seemed satisfied with that.
Rebecca went back to fixing the house. Max, as
usual, was studying.

It was a beautiful day, so Roxy decided to go
outside for a bit. Besides, the hawk might decide
to show up again. She may be grounded, but she
didn't plan on giving up on the case!

But instead of finding the hawk, Roxy found
a man on the front lawn. He wore an official-looking
uniform. He held a clipboard in his hand. A truck
was parked in the driveway with an official-looking
seal on it.

"Hello," he said when he saw Roxy.

"May I be so bold as to ask what you are doing here?" Roxy asked.

"You live here?" the man asked her.

"That is classified information," Roxy said. "Now before I summon the authorities, I will ask you once more. What are you doing here?"

The man smiled. "No need for the authorities. I'm Jefferson Hall. I'm a surveyor for the county," he explained. "I've been hired by the bank to survey this property for a proposed subdivision."

"May I see your credentials, please?" Roxy asked, in her most businesslike voice.

The man, like most adults, was startled by Roxy's directness. "What? Oh, yes," he said. He took out his wallet and showed Roxy his ID card. Roxy examined the official-looking seal of the County Works Department.

"Will that do?" the man asked.

"I suppose," Roxy replied. "My name's Roxy Hunter. I live here. Please excuse the necessary security protractions."

"You mean *precautions*?" The man chuckled. "Yes, absolutely. Would it be okay if I finished up?"

"Of course," Roxy replied. "Have a pleasant day, Mr. Hall."

The man nodded. "You too, miss."

Roxy walked back into the house. She found Max curled up in a chair, reading a book.

"Max, what's a subdivision?" she asked.

"It's like a bunch of houses," Max explained. "The suburbs, like back home."

"What's a surveyor?" Roxy asked next.

Max launched into a definition. "It's someone who does an overview of the topography of . . ."

"English, please," Roxy said.

"It's a guy who makes an official map," Max said. "Like if you're going to build a subdivision, a surveyor would have to map it out."

Roxy thought about this. Why would someone need to map out their land? What had Mr. Hall said . . . ?

"He said he was working for the bank!" Roxy cried.

She quickly ran up to her room. Something bad was brewing. Roxy knew it in her bones. She needed to make everyone understand, so she spent the next hour writing out the evil plot that she thought was underway. She drew pictures to illustrate what was happening. Then she ran downstairs to get Max.

She practically had to drag him into the room. But he came. He looked curiously at the pictures on the wall. One drawing showed stick figures of Max, Roxy, and Susan shivering outside the Moody Mansion. An evil-looking Jon was counting money.

The next drawing showed Max, Roxy, and Susan begging in the street. Jon lay on a sunny beach, surrounded by money.

The final drawing showed bulldozers pushing Max, Roxy, and Susan into a pile. Behind them, stick-figure workers built houses on the Moody property.

Roxy paced back and forth across the room.

"I think you'll find these scenarios fairly self-explanationary," Roxy said. "It is obvious that we have been lied to by the very evil Jon. It is clear now that he intends to fool my mother, then steal our house and put up a sub-decision. Oh, he's good. He's very good."

Max was not so sure. "I don't know," he said. "I'm sure there must be a logical explanation for this. And it's *self-explanatory*, not *self-explanationary*."

"Oh, there's an explanation, all right. But I'm afraid it might not be so logical.
And I intend to prove it," Roxy said firmly.

Max saw the determined look on Roxy's face.

He knew it could only mean one thing.

Trouble.

Max was right. Roxy knew she was grounded. But she *had* to prove to her mom that Jon was trying to steal their house away. It was a matter of life and—well, not having a place to live. And that was serious.

So Roxy snuck out once more. She wore a pair of Susan's sunglasses as a disguise. She pulled a hat across her face. Then she walked into town and watched the bank, hiding in some bushes.

Finally, Susan and Jon left the bank, headed for lunch. That's when Roxy made her move.

• • • ♥ • • •

Back at the Moody Mansion, Max was thoughtful. Roxy *did* have a big imagination. But it wasn't likely that she had dreamed up the surveyor and the subdivision plan. *Something* was going on. There had to be a logical explanation. So Max tried to find it.

He started with Rebecca. He found her in the basement. She wore safety goggles, and she was drilling through an old, steel door in the wall. She turned off the drill, and the door popped open. Behind the door was a small, empty room.

Rebecca frowned. Then she noticed Max on the stairs.

"Hey, Max. What's up?" she asked, suddenly cheerful again.

"Nothing. What are you doing?" Max asked.

"I was hoping to get the wiring all done for the house," she said. "I thought the schematics might have been in this old vault. Either that, or a million dollars."

She laughed, but Max didn't change his expression. There was something a little odd about her behavior . . .

Rebecca shifted under Max's uncomfortable stare. "What can I do for you, Max?" she asked.

"You are the estate lawyer for this property, correct?" Max asked.

"Yes," Rebecca replied.

"Well, Roxy said there was a surveyor here today," Max said. "Do you know anything about that?"

Rebecca looked surprised. "A surveyor? No, that's odd. Why would a surveyor be here?"

"That's what I was going to ask you," Max said.

"I . . . have no idea," Rebecca said carefully.

"He said he was hired by the bank. Maybe

Roxy Hunter: Super-Sleuth

The Moody Mansion

Whoa! A real-live haunted house

Clues in the attic

Madame Roxanne Dupuis d'Hunterre holds a séance

Roxy's ghost trap works—
It catches Ramma instead of a ghost

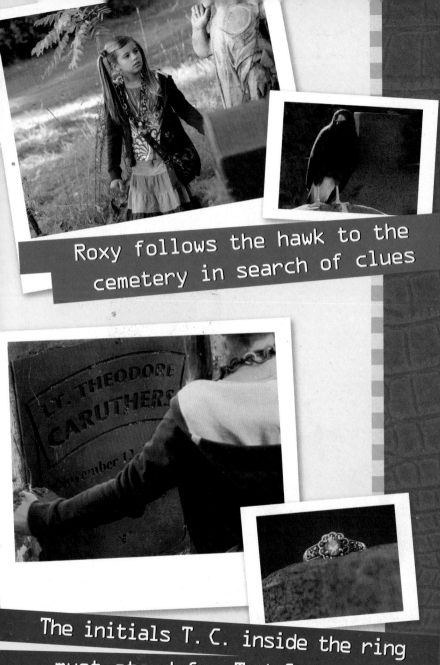

Roxy follows the hawk to the cemetery in search of clues

The initials T. C. inside the ring must stand for Ted Caruthers

Roxy and her mom have
a heart-to-heart

Roxy hunts for clues in Jon's office

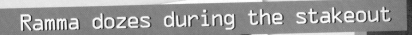
Ramma dozes during the stakeout

Roxy finally finds E. M.—
It's Estelle Moody

Roxy finds the real villain—
Rebecca

Mr. Middleton locks Max up

Rebecca's fake family dinner

Another case closed

Ted & Estelle—together again

Jon would know. I'll give him a call," Max said. He turned to go up the stairs.

"Hey, Max!" Rebecca cried. Max stopped. "You mind if I call? I'd feel kind of awkward explaining to my bosses that I got the information secondhand off a twelve-year-old. No offense."

"None taken," Max said.

Rebecca smiled. "Thanks, Max. You're the best."

Max headed up the stairs. *I'm sure there's a perfectly logical explanation,* he told himself.

But inside his head, a tiny voice told him something else.

Chapter Eleven:
• • • Big Trouble • • •

When Jon and Susan were out of sight,
Roxy walked into the bank. It wasn't very crowded.
The lady behind the teller window was busy with a
customer.

Roxy ducked behind a big potted plant next
to the door. She looked around the room. There was
a row of desks against the far wall. She scanned the
nameplates on the desks until she saw what she was
looking for: Jon Steadman.

She crawled across the floor and popped
up behind Jon's desk. As quietly as she could, she
opened one of the drawers. It was filled with files.
She started looking through them.

Soon she saw something familiar: a file with a
seal from the County Works Department. The same

seal on the surveyor's ID card. Inside the file was a letter from the surveyor!

"Gotcha red-handed!" Roxy whispered. She took the letter from the drawer and tucked it inside her jacket. Then she stood up and walked toward the door . . . right into a man in a suit and a woman with a sour look on her face.

"Why, hello, young lady. And how may we be of service?" the man asked.

"I'm Roxanne Hunter," Roxy said, thinking quickly. "Susan Hunter's daughter. I wanted to surprise Mom."

The man brightened. "Ah! Susan's little girl. I'm her boss, Mr. Middleton. And how are you settling in?"

"It's been illuminating, thank you," Roxy replied. She held her arm stiffly at her side, trying to make sure the file didn't fall out.

Mr. Middleton chuckled. "Illuminating? Ha-ha. What a pip."

The sour-faced woman was definitely not chuckling. "Your mother's not here," she said suspiciously, glancing at Mr. Middleton. "I think she's out for lunch. With Jon Steadman, I imagine."

"Guess you missed her," Middleton said,

kneeling down in fatherly gesture. "That reminds me of an old Middleton family saying: 'Don't go looking for something unless you're ready to find nothing.' Well, nice meeting you, Roxy."

The bank president stood up and walked away, but the woman squinted at Roxy.

"Your mother and Jon seem to be spending a lot of time together, don't they?" she asked.

Roxy didn't like Jon. But she wasn't about to get her mom in trouble. "Jon? I should definitely think not," Roxy said. "My mother is of unimpreacherable character, thank you. Have a nice day."

And without another word, she marched out of the bank, leaving the sour-faced woman speechless.

· · · ♥ · · ·

This time, Roxy got home before anyone noticed she was missing. She waited for her mom to get home, but it seemed like hours. She was anxious to see the look on her mom's face when she showed her the proof she had about Jon. But it had to be the perfect moment.

Finally, Susan came home. Roxy cornered her as Susan and Max set the dinner table.

"I notice you've set a place for Jon," Roxy said innocently.

"Yeah, honey, I told you that," Susan said. "He should be here in about a half hour."

"I think you'll want to reconsider that, after you've seen this!" Roxy dramatically held up the letter with the county seal on it. She placed it on the table.

"What is it?" Susan asked, puzzled.

"Incriminalating evidence," Roxy said.

"*Incriminating* evidence?" Susan asked.

"Yes. Today a surveyor from the bank came to sub-decide the property," Roxy continued.

"It's *subdivide*, Roxy, and yes, Max told me," Susan said. "I'm sure it's nothing, sweetie. Rebecca's handling it."

"Really?" Roxy asked. She held up the letter. "Mr. Hall from the county had a sign on his truck and on his badge. The same sign that I found on *this*!"

She thrust the letter in front of Susan's face. Susan looked it over.

"This is a survey report," she said.

"That I found in Jon's desk," Roxy said.

Susan looked shocked. "What? You went to the bank, snuck into Jon's office, and found this in his desk?"

83

"You will thank me later," Roxy said with certainty.

"Roxy, this is confidential information!" Susan said. Her face was flushed. "This is . . . this is theft!"

"I'm trying to save us!" Roxy said. "It's a survey report."

"Yes, it is," Susan said. "It's a survey of one-eighteen Walnut Crescent. That's on the other side of town!"

Roxy felt all the confidence leaking out of her. If that were true, she had made a pretty big mistake. "What?" she asked weakly.

"I can't believe you'd do such a thing!" Susan said. "Whatever were you thinking? Roxy, you've broken the law. You realize that, don't you?"

Just then, the phone rang. Max answered it.

"It's Jon," he said.

Susan glared at Roxy. "Don't move. Don't move and don't speak."

She walked to the phone. "Hey, Jon, something's happened, and I need to . . . what?"

Susan's face went pale. She took the phone into the hallway. When Susan came back, she looked miserable.

"Jon was suspended from the bank today," she said.

Roxy jumped up. "I knew it!" she cried. Jon was up to no good after all.

"Don't, Roxy. Don't!" Susan warned. "He was suspended because some anonymous person said he and I were dating. Roxy?"

"It wasn't me, Mom!" Roxy protested.

"How am I supposed to believe you?" Susan asked. "Roxy, we're talking about someone's job here."

"Mom, it wasn't me!"

"And not that it's anyone's concern, but Jon and I are just friends. Now, I want you up in your room right now," Susan said firmly.

"But I didn't do it!" Roxy yelled. She turned to Max. "You believe me, don't you?"

Max didn't answer.

"Your room, Roxy. Now," Susan said.

Roxy knew nothing she could say would matter. She turned and walked upstairs. Tears filled her eyes.

Her mom didn't believe her. Even Max didn't believe her.

She wasn't sure which hurt worse.

Chapter Twelve:

· · · A Villain Unmasked · · ·

Roxy spent the next hour crying in her room. The big purple box from the attic seemed to stare at her. Poor Estelle Moody and her lost love! Roxy knew what she must have felt like.

She wiped her tears and picked up the box. Then she took it into Max's bedroom.

"Love cannot live without trust, Max," she said. "How could I have been so foolish?"

She put the box on Max's bed.

"What is all this?" Max asked.

"Painful reminders of lost love," Roxy said. "Do with them what you will. The engagement is off. I'm sorry."

Roxy turned and made a dramatic exit through the doorway.

Then she heard Max's voice behind her.

"Hey! Roxy! Come here!" Max cried.

Roxy stuck her head back in the room. "It's no use, Max. Don't beg."

"I believe you, Roxy. You're right," Max said. He picked up a pink slip of paper on top of the box and waved it at her.

"You think Jon is an archfiend?" Roxy asked.

"No," Max said. "Not Jon."

Max told Roxy what he had figured out. The two talked late into the night, coming up with a plan to catch the real villain. Max would go to the mayor to present his evidence while Roxy would try to catch their suspect in the act. The next afternoon, Susan left them alone with Rebecca so she could run some errands. Roxy and Max were ready to put their plan into action.

Roxy looked out of the study window. She held a walkie-talkie in her hand.

"Heffalump, Heffalump, this is Winnie the Pooh. Do you copy?" Roxy asked.

There was no reply.

"Heffalump, do you copy?" Roxy asked. Still nothing. "Wake up, Ramma!"

Across the street, Ramma dozed in the driver's seat of a firewood delivery truck. He woke with a start at the sound of Roxy's voice.

"The left ventricle! The left!" he cried.

Then he remembered where he was, and what he was supposed to do. He rubbed his eyes. Then he picked up the walkie-talkie.

"This is Ramma," he replied.

"Please use your call name," Roxy said impatiently.

"Must I?" Ramma asked.

"It's for your own security," Roxy told him.

Ramma sighed. "This is Heffalump."

"Any sign of him?" Roxy asked. Max was on a mission—part of their plan. He should have been back by now.

"No, I do not see him," Ramma said.

"Well, we'll start without him," Roxy said.

"Oh, no, no, no," Ramma said. "Max was quite adamant that we do not commence until his return." Ramma paused. "Would it be an imposition at this time to ask just what exactly is going to commence?"

Roxy shook her head. They needed someone who could drive, and Ramma had agreed to help them, no questions asked. And that's how it needed to stay.

"No can do. Security reasons," Roxy replied. "Pooh out."

She turned off her walkie-talkie. "Come on, Maxie," she said anxiously. "Where are you?"

· · · ♥ · · ·

Max was actually in Peter Middleton's office. Not his office at the bank, but in his mayor's office.

When Max saw the piece of pink paper, he knew Roxy was right about one thing: Someone was selling the Moody property. The paper was a deed to the Moody land—a piece of paper that said who owned the property. Max had looked on the Internet and discovered that someone was trying to make the sale in secret. He had come to the mayor's office to find out more. The mayor had asked to speak to him.

"When Cheryl told me a young man wanted access to the county records, I thought it was for a school project," Middleton said. "I had no idea . . ."

"It's all there, Mr. Mayor," Max said. "Someone has taken all the necessary steps to build a massive new neighborhood on the Moody land. They've procured zoning approval, public works projections, everything. The actual purchase of the Moody land is the only piece missing. The deal can't go through without it."

"Well, it all seems legal," Middleton said.

Max shook his head. "No, sir. The company that represents the Moody estate isn't registered. I checked the records. It's a ghost company."

"How do you know all this?" Middleton asked.

Max shrugged. "The Internet."

Middleton thought for a moment. "You and I had best take this to Tom, our sheriff."

"No, sir," Max said. "With all due respect, the police can't do anything yet. There's been no hard crime committed."

"Then what do you suggest?" Middleton asked.

Max leaned forward. "I am currently running a covert operation that I believe will connect the perpetrator to the crime," he said. He looked at his watch. "An operation that I'm late for."

Middleton stroked his chin. "Then let's get to the bottom of this," he said. "We'll take my car."

· · · ♥ · · ·

Back at the Moody Mansion, Roxy paced back and forth across the study. What was taking Max so long? Then she saw Rebecca walk past the door. She wore her coat.

"Where are you going?" Roxy asked, following her.

"I've got an appointment in town," Rebecca said. "I'll be back for dinner tonight. Will you tell Max to hold down the fort?"

Roxy had to think quickly. Max or no Max, she had to begin phase two.

"Wait! You can't go now. I need your help," Roxy said. She ran to the hall closet and pulled out the purple box.

"I'm in a rush, Roxy," Rebecca said.

"Only take a sec," Roxy said. "I found this stuff and I was wondering if it'd be okay to make a festive collage for your birthday."

"What is it?" Rebecca asked, tapping her foot.

"Just some stuff from the attic," Roxy said casually.

That caught Rebecca's interest. "You found a way into the attic?"

"Yeah," Roxy replied.

Rebecca walked over to the box. She spotted the pink slip on top, and her eyes grew wide. She quickly snatched it up.

"It was in the attic," Rebecca whispered. "In the attic."

Rebecca slowly turned to Roxy. "You know, I really think it would be best if you came with me," she said in a sweet voice. "Technically I'm supposed to be babysitting. It'll be fun. Two girls on the town. What do you say?"

Roxy tried to act cool. Leaving the house with Rebecca was definitely *not* part of phase two.

"I'd love to!" Roxy lied. Then she frowned. "Oh, flibbersnibbets. I'm grounded. Too bad, but rules are rules."

Roxy pretended to hear something. "Is that Max calling me? I'd better go. See you tonight!"

Roxy quickly bounded up the stairs. Rebecca started to follow her, but her cell phone rang. She checked the number, then put the phone to her ear.

"I got it! I finally got it!" she said. Then she glanced up the stairs. A smile crossed her face, but it wasn't her usual cheerful one. It was the smile of a cat about to pounce on a mouse.

"I just have to grab the kid."

Chapter Thirteen:
• • • A Dastardly Deed • • •

Peter Middleton was talking into his cell phone. He sat in the driver's seat of his car. Max sat in the passenger seat.

"That's fantastic news," he said. "And don't worry. I've got young Max in the car."

On the other end of the phone, Rebecca smiled. "Really? Then we don't need the girl. I'll see you tonight."

Rebecca put her cell phone back into her pocket, and left the Moody Mansion.

Max had no idea Middleton was talking to Rebecca. But that little voice inside him was talking again. And it was telling him that something definitely wasn't right.

"Who was that?" he asked.

"Susan," the mayor lied. "Just checking in with her at the bank."

"But it's Saturday," Max said carefully. "Isn't the bank closed?"

"Just to the public, Max," Middleton said. "Money doesn't take a holiday."

The little voice inside Max was screaming now. He had been sure that Rebecca was plotting to steal the Moody property. But she would have to have had help. Powerful help.

"It occurs to me that those plans were okayed by your office," Max said slowly. "And the financing was arranged by your bank. But you never ran a check on that ghost corporation."

Middleton started the car, and Max got a sick feeling in his stomach.

"We're not going home, are we?" Max asked.

Middleton clicked the automatic car door locks into place and smiled. "No, we're not."

. . . ♥ . . .

Back at the Moody house, Roxy watched Rebecca drive off. This was bad—really bad. She ran downstairs, out of the house, and across the street. Then she climbed into the truck next to Ramma.

"The chicken has flown!" Roxy cried.

Ramma looked puzzled.

"The goose is loose!"

Ramma still didn't move.

"Follow Rebecca!" Roxy yelled.

"I have been given strict instructions to wait for Max," Ramma said.

Roxy gave Ramma her fiercest look. Ramma sighed. He knew Roxy had him. "Very well," he said, starting the truck. "We roll like stones with no moss."

Ramma tore down the street after Rebecca.

· · · ♥ · · ·

On the other side of town, Susan had no idea that a plan was underway. She had a mistake to fix. She drove to Jon's house and was relieved when he let her in.

"Roxy is having a difficult time adjusting to a lot of things," Susan explained. "And I think she may have thought you and I were dating and accidentally told someone that she thought so . . ."

"It wasn't Roxy," Jon said, smiling as he interrupted her. "I checked into it. And weirdly, it wasn't Crabtree, either. I'm going to sort this out tomorrow. It's all pretty ridiculous."

Susan sighed with relief. "I'm so happy to

hear that. You know, we're having a housewarming dinner tonight, and I'm hopeless at making gravy. Could you come over and help me out?"

Jon smiled. "I'll give it a shot."

· · · ♥ · · ·

On the other side of town, Ramma and Roxy raced after Rebecca's car.

"Would it be a terrible imposition to ask exactly what you have involved me in?" Ramma asked. "My friend Jon went to great troubles to get me this job delivering firewood, and I would like to know, before I am freshly fired for misuse of company property."

Roxy knew she couldn't keep the truth from Ramma any longer. "Max says that Rebecca hasn't really been working on the house. She's been looking for something. A piece of paper I found, called a deed," Roxy explained. "I always thought a deed was a good thing you do—like helping old ladies across the street, or feeding peanut brittle to homeless cats."

"Peanut brittle? I'm very sorry, but you are making no sense to me," Ramma said. "I am just a simple med student who has not slept properly in two weeks."

"With that piece of paper, Rebecca can steal the Moody house and turn it into a sub-decision!" Roxy said.

"She is going to steal the house? What a dastardly woman indeed!" Ramma chuckled at his own joke. "Get it? In-*deed*!"

Roxy just rolled her eyes. Ramma might not be a comedian, but he was a great driver. He caught up to Rebecca. Then he slowed down as Rebecca pulled into a circular driveway. Roxy read the sign in front of the white building.

"Shady Oak Retirement Home?" she wondered.

"I believe it is an institute where elderly people live," Ramma suggested.

He parked the truck across from the retirement home as Rebecca walked into the building.

"What does she need with an elderly person?" Roxy wondered. "I'm going to check it out. You wait here."

"I am sorry, young Roxy, but I cannot allow you to go into some strange establishment on your own," Ramma said. "I will come with you."

Roxy rolled her eyes. "Ramma, this is America. In America detectives detect, and drivers drive. That's how it works. You have to stay in the truck in case she gives me the slip."

Before he could say anything, she was out of the car and running to the door of the retirement home. He shrugged helplessly.

Roxy marched inside and walked past the front desk, smiling brightly at the nurse there.

"Hello, are you looking for someone?" the nurse asked.

"Yes, I'm looking for my grandma," Roxy lied.

"Well, tell me what her name is, and I'll let you know what room she's in," the nurse offered.

Roxy was stuck. "Her name? Gosh, I don't know!"

She cringed. That was not the answer she should have given.

"You don't know her name?" the nurse asked.

Roxy thought quickly. "Well, she's had so many of them."

The nurse was really puzzled now. Roxy leaned over the desk.

"Granny was a spy," she said in a loud whisper. "Don't tell anyone. Could be deadly in the wrong hands, if you know what I mean. But don't worry, I'll know her when I see her."

The nurse wasn't buying it. "Where are your parents?" she asked suspiciously.

"Outside," Roxy said.

"Well, maybe you should stay here until they show up," the nurse suggested.

Roxy looked down the hall. "No need. There she is. Granny!" she cried.

She ran down the hall, hoping the nurse wouldn't follow. She turned a corner, and then slowed down. She wanted to find Rebecca, but she didn't want Rebecca to find *her*. She flattened herself against the wall and cautiously made her way down the hall. She peered into every open door.

In room after room she saw people sleeping, sitting, and eating. But no Rebecca. In the next room she checked, she saw an elderly woman talking with a nurse. The window behind them was open, and sitting on a tree branch outside was the hawk!

The bird screeched loudly. Roxy froze by the door. He wanted her to pay attention. She saw that the elderly woman was signing something. Something pink.

"The deed," Roxy whispered.

The nurse put the paper in her pocket and then turned, facing the door. Now Roxy could clearly see her face. It was Rebecca in disguise!

Roxy dove behind a cart in the hallway containing a pile of sheets. She draped one of the sheets over herself and held her breath. Rebecca walked right past without noticing her.

When she was sure the coast was clear, Roxy tiptoed into the room. The elderly woman looked up at her.

"Hello," she said.

"Are you Rebecca's accomplish?" Roxy asked.

"I'm sorry, what?" the woman asked.

"Her partner in crime," Roxy explained.

The woman frowned. "Oh . . . *accomplice.* Wait, who's Rebecca?"

Roxy wasn't sure what to say or do. Who was this woman, and what did she have to do with Rebecca's plan? She looked out the window, but the hawk was gone.

"Sorry to bother you," Roxy said.

"No bother," the woman said. "It's nice to have visitors. I'm Estelle. What's your name?"

Roxy's eyes widened. "Estelle? Estelle Moody?"

Estelle looked surprised. "Estelle Moody? Oh, my gracious. I haven't heard that name in years! Yes, I guess I am—was."

"But you're supposed to be dead," Roxy said.

"Well, a little tired, but not there yet, thank you," Estelle said. "Now what is this all about?"

A voice piped up from behind the door. "Exactly my question."

Roxy turned to see Rebecca in the doorway. She didn't look like the cheerful Rebecca who came to their house every day. She looked mean, and deadly serious.

Rebecca forced Estelle and Roxy out of the room. The front-desk nurse had left her post, so Rebecca was able to take them outside. Roxy looked at the firewood truck. Ramma had to see what was happening! He would come to their rescue! He would . . .

But Ramma was fast asleep.

Chapter Fourteen:
· · · A Nasty Threat · · ·

The sun was setting and the air was getting chilly as Mayor Middleton led Max into the little cemetery in the woods. He held Max by the arm, pulling him past headstones bathed in shadows.

Max was terrified, but he tried not to show it.

"I really can't figure out how you plan on getting away with this, sir," Max said.

"Respectability, Max," Middleton replied, cackling. "Never underestimate the power of a respectable image."

He stopped in front of the Middleton family tomb and pushed open the heavy door, letting out a *whoosh* of musty air.

Max peered inside. The tomb was filled with rotting wood caskets covered with spiderwebs. He shivered.

"In you go, Maxie," Middleton said gruffly. "And remember, you play fair, and nothing happens to little Roxy."

Max stepped inside the tomb. Middleton closed the door behind him. Then he locked the door with a padlock.

Max looked around in the gloom, listening as Middleton's footsteps walked away.

It's only a tomb, Max told himself. *There's nothing here that can hurt you.*

He took a deep breath. Roxy and Ramma knew he had gone to the mayor's office. They'd figure out where he was. Roxy especially. She never gave up, right? That was the good thing about Roxy.

And right now, it was the only hope he had.

· · · · · ·

Over at the Moody house, Jon walked through the front door holding a packet of gravy mix.

"Hello? The gravy train has arrived," he called out.

But when he walked into the kitchen, he found Susan sitting at the table, where a delicious looking meal waited. She looked upset.

"Great," she said. "Now we have everything except for . . . the children!"

"Both of them?" Jon asked.

"I have no idea where they are. There's no note, no message," Susan said, her voice full of despair. She sighed. "Is there a law against keeping children locked in the basement?"

"I think it varies from state to state," Jon joked. "Do you want me to take a drive around and look for them?"

"No, that's okay," Susan said, trying to convince herself. "If Roxy's with Max, I'm sure they're fine."

"Actually, they're not," a voice said from the doorway.

Susan and Jon turned to see Rebecca, with Roxy and a very confused Estelle Moody on either side of her.

"Mom, this really isn't my fault," Roxy said.

"What's going on?" Susan asked, jumping to her feet and rushing to Roxy's side.

"What's going on is that I'm about to make a lot of money selling this old heap of a house. And you and your nosy brats aren't going to ruin this for me—I've made sure of that," Rebecca snarled, yanking Roxy and Estelle into the kitchen. "Now let's finish setting the table. This is supposed to be a party."

A few minutes later, Rebecca glared at them over the feast spread out on the dining room table.

"All right, the developer is on his way here," she told them. "As far as he's concerned, we're all a nice family, having a nice dinner—in *my* house. You cooperate, and nothing bad happens to Max. Right now he's locked up somewhere safe, but if you try to ruin this he won't be safe for long."

She held up her cell phone. "So start piling food on your plates. Remember, all I have to do is press send, text message my partner, and it's bye-bye Max. Got it?"

"You wouldn't dare!" Roxy said angrily.

"I can give you twelve million reasons why I would," Rebecca replied.

Estelle looked bewildered. "Just for this old house?"

"No, I'm guessing for the land," Jon said.

"Bingo," Rebecca said. "We recently learned the best-kept secret in Serenity Falls. The original Moody purchase included the surrounding woods— all one hundred and twenty acres."

"Oh my," Estelle said.

"All prime residential suburbs," Rebecca said smugly. "Hundreds and hundreds of sweet little cookie-cutter homes."

"But you'll tear down all the trees!" Roxy said.

"It's called progress. Get over it," Rebecca said. "It's all ours now, anyway, thanks to Estelle's signature. And when Mr. Franklin comes and gives me a nice big check, it'll be his. Now be quiet and eat!"

Rebecca's captives slowly picked at their food. Rebecca walked to the window, restless.

Roxy leaned over and whispered to Estelle, "Why did you give her the house?"

"I thought she was selling it for me. It was too big for me on my own," Estelle said. "I can't believe I was so foolish as to have trusted her."

"But why have us live here?" Susan wondered out loud.

"After nine years, an unoccupied house becomes property of the county," Jon explained. "I'm guessing she needed someone in here fast."

A car pulled into the driveway. Rebecca turned back to them.

"Showtime," she said. "Now, anyone—and I mean anyone—says anything out of line, and Max becomes part of family history."

Roxy's stomach tightened at the mention of Max. As soon as that man gave Rebecca the check, they didn't know what might happen. They needed time.

"You'll never get away with this, Rebecca," Roxy said angrily.

Rebecca grinned. "I probably wouldn't—if my real name were Rebecca."

"Oh. What is your real name?" Roxy asked.

"Nice try, sweetheart," Rebecca replied.

There was a knock on the door.

"Remember, happy family," Rebecca warned them. She walked to the front door.

"Please, everyone, do as she says," Susan said. "It's not worth jeopardizing Max."

Then Roxy heard a sound from the window. A pecking sound. She turned—to see the hawk!

It didn't make sense. Roxy had always thought that the hawk was Estelle Moody's spirit form. But Estelle wasn't dead.

"It must be Ted," Roxy said to herself.

"Roxy, do you hear me? No heroics, no

detecting, nothing. Understood?" Susan asked urgently.

Roxy nodded. "Yeah, sure."

She looked in the doorway to see Rebecca talking to a short, balding man. He was looking over the deed.

"Everything seems to be in order," he said. He handed Rebecca an envelope. "Here's your cashier's check. Congratulations."

Rebecca pulled the check out of the envelope. There was a look of awe on her face.

"Wow, I've never seen so many zeroes in my life," she said eagerly. Mr. Franklin gave her a suspicious look. Rebecca sure didn't sound like the sweet, small-town girl he thought she was.

Rebecca slipped back into her sweet homeowner act, stammering out, "The money is great, but still, it's going to be sad leaving here. So many memories." As Rebecca talked, the hawk kept pecking at the window. Ted was trying to tell Roxy something. But what?
Roxy needed more time.

"Well, I'm off," Mr. Franklin said. He turned and waved to everyone at the table. "So long!"

"Why don't you join us?" Roxy said quickly.

"What?" Rebecca and Susan asked at the same time.

Roxy knew she had Rebecca beat—for now. If Rebecca wanted them to act like a happy family, that's exactly what she would do.

"The poor man must be famished," Roxy said. "And doesn't our happy family pride itself on its hospitality?"

Mr. Franklin looked pleased—and hungry. "Well, I tell you, I wouldn't mind a slice of that sweet potato pie I see on the table."

Rebecca glared at Roxy, but she didn't want to give anything away. Susan just shook her head.

Roxy smiled as brightly as she could.

· · · ♥ · · ·

Back at the retirement home, Ramma sprang awake. Darkness had fallen. Rebecca's car was gone. And there was no sign of Roxy.

"Oh no," Ramma said, starting the engine. "This is very bad!"

Chapter Fifteen:
· · · Roxy Saves the Day · · ·

All eyes in the room were on Mr. Franklin as he swallowed his last bite of sweet potato pie.

"My goodness, that was good," he remarked.

Roxy grabbed a bowl of beans. She held out the plate to him.

"Here, have some greens," she said.

"No!" Everyone responded at once.

Mr. Franklin was startled. "I didn't realize I was imposing. I'll be leaving, then."

Roxy was desperate to buy more time. She didn't think Rebecca would do anything while Mr. Franklin was still there. She didn't want to ruin her deal.

"No, no, no," Roxy said sweetly. "It's just a little game we play. If you mention the color green, it's a five-point deduction."

She leaned in to Mr. Franklin and lowered

her voice. "Whatever you do, don't say 'purple.' Automatic fifty."

Susan was afraid that Roxy might be angering Rebecca. She didn't want to endanger Max.

"Roxy, honey, we don't want to force-feed Mr. Franklin here," she said. "I think he's been gracious enough."

"Yes," Rebecca said, glaring at Roxy. "Remember what happened to cousin Max when you made him eat all that food. We had to lock him someplace scary until he starved himself slim. Don't go looking for something unless you're ready to find trouble."

Roxy knew Rebecca was giving her a warning. But she wasn't ready to give up yet. "Don't be silly, Mr. Franklin is . . ."

Roxy froze. She closed her eyes, deep in thought. There was something familiar about what Rebecca had just said. Her mind leapt back to the day she had met Peter Middleton at the bank.

"*That reminds me of an old Middleton family saying: 'Don't go looking for something unless you're ready to find nothing.'*"

Rebecca and Middleton must be connected somehow. But this wasn't the first time she had been warned about Peter Middleton, was it? The day the hawk led her to the cemetery, it perched on a tomb.

A tomb marked "Middleton."

Rebecca had said something else, too. *"We had to lock him someplace scary until he starved..."*

The Middleton tomb. Someplace scary. It all made sense now.

Roxy's eyes popped open. "I know where Max is," she said.

Everyone at the table was shocked. "What?"

"And I know who she is," Roxy said, nodding toward Rebecca. "Her last name's Middleton. Like the man at the bank."

"Mr. Middleton?" Jon and Susan blurted out at the same time, surprised.

Just then, the glare of blue and red police lights shone through the windows. Help was on the way. Roxy felt like cheering, but then Rebecca stood up. She held up her cell phone.

"Nobody move," she ordered.

"What is going on here?" Mr. Franklin asked.

"Nothing, fatso. Just a kid's life is at

stake," Rebecca snapped. She looked at Susan and Jon. "What if she's wrong? You willing to take that risk? Now you keep quiet to the cops, and I'll call with Max's location in half an hour. Play it cool, or he gets maxed out."

Roxy didn't take her eyes off of Rebecca for a second. The woman was standing right under the busted spot in the ceiling. Roxy could see a chunk of plaster hanging, already loose.

She had an idea.

"Now, Ted, now!" Roxy cried.

At her words, the hawk cawed loudly and a large chunk of plaster fell from the ceiling.

WHACK! The chunk fell directly on Rebecca's head.

She dropped the cell phone and then crumpled to the floor in a heap.

Chapter Sixteen:
· · · Case Closed! · · ·

Not long after, Rebecca was in the custody of the police. Susan, Jon, and Estelle stood outside as Ramma explained his part in the story.

"When I awoke, I knew that I must be calling the police at once," he said.

"It's lucky they got here when they did," Jon said gratefully.

Estelle glanced at Rebecca, who was being led to a police car in handcuffs.

"Roberta Middleton," she said, shaking her head. "I can't believe it. Didn't recognize Peter's daughter at all. She was shipped off when she was very young. Always was a bad apple."

"Guess it didn't fall too far from the family tree," Jon added.

As they talked, a new police cruiser pulled into the driveway. A sheriff got out and opened the back door. Max emerged, wrapped in a blanket.

"He's fine. Just a little shaken up," the sheriff said.

Roxy ran up to him and hugged him tightly.

"I knew they'd find you! I knew it!" She squeezed him again. Roxy talked fast. "I was so frightened, but I knew Ted was trying to tell me something, even though everyone wanted me to be quiet and eat. I knew I'd figure it out. And I'll never break off the engagement again."

"Um, okay," Max said awkwardly.

Susan ran up and hugged them both.

"You all right?" she asked Max, concerned.

He nodded. "All things considered, yeah."

Roxy was thrilled to see Max again. But the case wasn't quite closed yet. There was still part of the story she needed to hear—the story of Estelle Moody and Ted Caruthers.

Susan invited everyone back inside. Jon started a fire in the fireplace. Roxy, Max, Susan,

Jon, and Ramma gathered around Estelle, who sat in a comfortable armchair. They listened to her story intently.

"My father thought Ted was too poor," Estelle began. "But Ted and I decided to get married anyway, before he was shipped off to Europe. I was to be Mrs. Theodore Caruthers."

Estelle got a dreamy look in her eyes as she remembered that night long ago. "I thought my dad would let us marry once he saw how handsome Ted looked in his uniform. He came to the house one night. Father wouldn't let him in, but Ted came in anyway. I was upstairs in my room. I heard them argue, and then a gunshot rang out."

Roxy gasped.

"I screamed and ran down the stairs," Estelle said. "I expected the worst. But Father and Ted were still standing. My father was covered in white dust, and he held a shotgun in his hand. He had blown a hole in the ceiling."

Estelle cast a glance at the dining room. Roxy couldn't believe it. It was the very same spot that the plaster chunk kept falling from!

"To his dying day, my father swore it was an accident. He never meant to fire the gun," Estelle continued, shaking her head. "But Ted didn't want us to get married that way. He promised he'd come back for me. No matter what, he'd come back."

A sad look crossed Estelle's face. She gazed into the fire. "Three days later, his ship was torpedoed in the Atlantic. I never saw Ted again."

Roxy's eyes filled with tears. She knew what that was like—to never see someone again.

"Life goes on," Estelle said quietly. "I didn't think it would, but it does. I married a lovely man and we had a wonderful life together, but I never forgot Ted. And I don't think I should have. There was always a part of me that belonged to him."

Susan nodded, giving a sad smile. Roxy looked at her mother, then at Jon.

"I guess the life going on part isn't so bad," Roxy said softly.

"No, dear, it's wonderful," Estelle assured her.

Susan and Jon looked at each other. Ramma wiped tears from his eyes.

"I'm sorry, but that is just so beautiful," he said. He blew his nose loudly on a napkin.

Everyone laughed.

Estelle agreed to stay the night, and Roxy was happy to give up her room. She also had one more thing to give to Estelle. Roxy knocked on her bedroom door.

Estelle opened it, wearing an old, white nightgown. She smiled when she saw Roxy.

Roxy held out the engagement ring she had found.

"I thought you should have this," she said.

Estelle took the ring. She held it in her palm. A wistful smile crossed her face.

"Does this mean we have to move now?" Roxy asked.

"No, dear," Estelle replied. "In fact, I've already taken steps to make sure you can stay here as long as you want. It's so nice to have a family in this house."

Roxy hugged her. "Thank you, Estelle."

"No, thank you, Roxy."

Roxy left the room and closed the door behind her. She walked back down to the living room and climbed onto the couch, staring at the dying flames of the fire. They had only been here a week, and so much had happened. She had made new friends—both hawk and human—and solved some mysteries. Things were going to seem pretty boring after that.

Then Roxy grinned. She had a feeling that things would never get boring in her new home. There would always be new people to meet, and new mysteries to solve.

And Roxy would be ready for them.

"Life goes on," she whispered.

Epilogue
The Present

Every haunted house has a story. If you had been inside the Moody house that night, you would have seen that story come to an end . . .

Estelle Moody sleeps peacefully in Roxy's bed. Her eyes flutter open. She looks around the dark room. Standing by the window is a tall man in an army uniform.

It's Ted.

Ted smiles at Estelle, and she looks at him in awe. He walks over to her and kneels beside the bed.

"I said I'd come back to you, didn't I?" he whispers.

He takes the engagement ring from the

bedside table and places it on her finger. The wrinkles in Estelle's hand fade away.

Estelle stands and looks in the mirror. A beautiful young woman stares back at her. She is no longer old and she is dressed in her wedding gown. Ted takes her hand.

Downstairs, Roxy Hunter opens her eyes. She looks up to the balcony. She sees Estelle and Ted on the balcony, gazing into each other's eyes. They lean in and give each other a kiss. A kiss that has waited sixty years.

Then their ghostly figures start to shimmer. They slowly fade into the night.

Roxy smiles . . .

Every haunted house has a story.

And if you are lucky enough to have Roxy Hunter on the case, you can be sure that the story will have a happy ending!

• • • ♥ • • •

Don't miss the next adventure in the series!

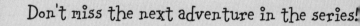

Roxy Hunter and the Secret of the Shaman

Eleven-year-old Andy walked nervously across the marsh.

It was late, and only the white moon overhead lit his way. The dark woods ringing the marsh seemed to be closing in on him.

A low wind rustled the tall grass. It sounded like ghostly whispers.

Then thunder rumbled in the distance, warning of a coming storm.

Andy stopped and listened. *Was* that thunder he had heard? Or was it the roar of some strange . . .

Whoooooooo!

Andy jumped. He looked around, panicked now.

An owl flew past him. Andy breathed a sigh of relief.

It's only an owl, he told himself. *Just keep going and you'll be home soon.*

Andy forged ahead.

Creeeeeeeeeak!

He froze again, nearly paralyzed with fear this time. That sound was definitely not an owl.

A new sound crept across the marsh. It came from the woods: the sound of twigs snapping.

Someone was coming.

"H-h-hello?" Andy called out nervously. He was beginning to regret taking the shortcut. Every kid in Serenity Falls knew the Legend of the Black Marsh Monster. People had been claiming they'd heard strange sounds and seen a monstrous figure in the marsh for years. But Andy had never believed it—at least not until tonight.

"Anybody there?" he called out, his voice croaking.

But nobody answered.

It's just your imagination, Andy told himself. *Just your imagination. Just your imagination . . .*

He repeated the chant and walked on.

Then a huge figure ran out of the woods. The monstrous, hunched form blocked the path ahead.

"Aaaaaaaaaaaah!" Andy screamed louder than he had ever screamed in his life. He turned and ran back down the trail.

Andy took the long way home that night.